A Christmas for Katie

By Shelley Shepard Gray

Sisters of the Heart series
Hidden
Wanted
Forgiven
Grace

Seasons of Sugarcreek series
Winter's Awakening
Spring's Renewal
Autumn's Promise
Christmas in Sugarcreek

Families of Honor
The Caregiver
The Protector
The Survivor
A Christmas for Katie (novella)

The Secrets of Crittenden County
Missing
The Search
Found

SHELLEY SHEPARD GRAY

....

A CHRISTMAS FOR KATIE

A Christmas
Families of Honor Novella

AVON
INSPIRE

A CHRISTMAS FOR KATIE. Copyright © 2012 by Shelley Shepard Gray. All rights reserved under International and Pan-American Copyright Conventions. By payment of the required fees, you have been granted the nonexclusive, nontransferable right to access and read the text of this e-book on screen. No part of this text may be reproduced, transmitted, decompiled, reverse-engineered, or stored in or introduced into any information storage and retrieval system, in any form or by any means, whether electronic or mechanical, now known or hereinafter invented, without the express written permission of HarperCollins e-books.

EPub Edition DECEMBER 2012 ISBN: 9780062242549
Print Edition ISBN: 9780062242563

10 9 8 7 6 5 4 3 2

I tell you the truth, if you had faith even as small as a mustard seed, you could say to this mountain, "Move from here to there," and it would move. Nothing would be impossible.

MATTHEW 17:20

Even if something don't seem like much, someone might think differently. Ain't so?

KATIE WEAVER, AGE 6½

Chapter One

· · · · · · · · ·

IT WAS A difficult thing, being Katie Weaver. At six and a half years old, she was about to be an aunt for the second time! But that was what happened when a girl had three much older married brothers, she supposed. After a while, they wanted to start families of their own.

Her brothers were good to her, and her new sisters were *wonderful-gut*, too. As was Mamm—when she wasn't complaining about Katie driving her crazy.

But at the moment, Katie felt alone. No one seemed to care that the Christmas nativity was in danger of falling apart—right in front of their town's eyes.

Staring at the front lawn of the Jacob's Crossing Public Library, she glared at the run-down crèche, broken wooden cradle, and ten plastic figures that had probably been peeling paint since before her oldest brother, Calvin, was born. Crossing her arms underneath the heavy black cloak that her *mamm* had just made for her, she grumbled, "This won't do. It won't do at all."

"What won't do?" Ella Weaver, her favorite sister-in-law, asked.

Katie started. She'd thought Ella had gone inside a full five minutes ago. But though she'd thought she was talking to herself, she might as well be honest. "*None* of it." When Ella tilted her head to one side looking like she didn't hear her correctly, Katie cleared her throat and tried not to sound so whiney. "I mean, this whole nativity ain't right. None of it is."

Ella bent down to look at her in that patient, serious way she always did. "And what is wrong with the nativity, child?"

"To start with, it's all worn down and old. Plus, it's plastic." Though that, of course, was mighty obvious.

Turning away from the plastic figures, she added, "Ella, what we need is a *real* nativity."

"You think so, hmm?"

"*Jah*. With real people and animals. Not cracked and broken-down plastic ones."

Ella tilted her head and eyed her quietly for a moment. Katie was sure she was going to use that *precocious* word people said to her so often. But instead, her sister-in-law nodded her head.

"A nativity scene made up of real people would be mighty special, for sure," Ella said solemnly. "But it would be quite an undertaking. I don't know too many people who want to stand out here for hours on end dressed like shepherds or wise men."

"Not even to be Mary or Joseph?"

"Not even Mary or Joseph, I'm afraid. This has been a particularly cold and snowy December. Even Mary and Joseph sought shelter in a stable, yes?"

Her expression softening, Ella pressed a mittened hand on the back of Katie's neck, just under the edge of her white *kapp* and black bonnet. "But I think I see your point, dear. Perhaps Loyal or Graham can get out their tools and fix things up. It does look as if a big wind could blow it all down."

Having her brothers do repairs would be a definite improvement. But it wasn't exactly what she wanted. "What do you think Miss Donovan would say if I asked her if real people could take the plastic people's spots, just for one night?"

"Just for one night, hmm? Perhaps on Christmas Eve?"

Katie nodded, glad that she and Ella were thinking along the same lines. "Jah. That seems the best night for the nativity, don't you think?"

Ella stared at her hard, then shrugged. "You know, I don't think it would hurt to ask. Let's go inside and see what Jayne has to say."

Feeling a fresh burst of happiness, Katie reached for Ella's hand and walked by her side into the library. Over a year ago, her sister-in-law had taken a job at the library, and now she was the children's librarian. This was when Katie had first joined the summer reading club and had become a frequent visitor to the library, too. Both she and Ella had also become good friends with Miss Donovan, the head librarian.

When they got inside, the warm air of the library felt like a welcome caress after the freezing temperatures outside. Ella stretched her arms a bit and unbuttoned the top button of her winter cloak. With the cloak unfastened, Ella's tummy looked even bigger than it usually did. "It feels much better in here, Katie," she murmured quietly as they passed several groups of patrons, both Amish and English, as they walked toward the circulation desk.

But while nine times out of ten, that was where you'd find Miss Donovan, the chair she usually sat in was empty.

Katie looked this way and that. "Where could she be, Ella?"

"No telling. Let's just be patient . . . ah, there she is."

Katie followed Ella's gaze and smiled brightly. Miss Donovan was standing in the middle of the nonfiction section. Her reading glasses were on, and she was kind of hunched over, reading one of the books intently. She snapped to attention when Katie called her name.

"Hi, Katie. I didn't know you two were stopping by today."

"Katie needed another book," Ella said with a laugh. "Plus, the *doktah* said getting out of the *haus* is *gut* for me."

"Ella's gonna have a *boppli*," Katie explained. Maybe a little too loudly.

Ella's cheeks turned the color of the cranberries in her mother's glass bowl. "Katie, hush!"

"Sorry. Anyway, Miss Donovan, me and Ella need to talk to you about something."

After setting her book and reading glasses on one of the metal shelves, Miss Donovan raised a brow. "About what?"

"About the ugly nativity outside. I think we need real people instead of plastic."

The librarian looked taken aback. "Well, now . . ."

Pressing on Katie's shoulder, Ella cleared her throat. "Katie didn't mean to be hurtful, did you, dear?"

Knowing what that firm hand meant, Katie shook her head. "No, Miss D."

Looking pleased, Ella continued, "She was merely telling me outside how *wunderbaar* a real nativity would be for one night."

"*Jah*. Just for Christmas Eve," Katie said importantly.

The librarian's pretty violet eyes softened. "Well, now that would be something, wouldn't it?" She paused, gazed at the cover of the book she'd just set down, then shook her head. "I'm sorry. I wouldn't know the first thing about how to set that up. I don't think I'm up for it this year, either. But we should keep it in mind for next Christmas."

Katie couldn't bear to let her idea get tossed away like yesterday's trash. "But, Miss D., it wouldn't be hard. I'd find all the people for it."

"That's all well and good, but they'd need costumes."

"I bet Ella and my other sisters-in-law could help with them. Right, Ella?"

"I suppose we could," Ella said, with a twinkle in her eye.

Miss Donovan smiled, but after a moment shook her head. "As I said, maybe next year. I'm afraid I'm not up for doing one more thing this Christmas season."

"But—"

Ella pressed her shoulder again. Hard enough for Katie to realize that it was time to stop with her pestering. "Katie, we asked," she said firmly. "Now let's let Miss Donovan have some privacy, *jah*?"

Katie didn't argue, Even she knew when it was *really* time to stop. But she couldn't help but hang her head the whole time they left the building.

Her brother Loyal was waiting for them in his buggy when they stumbled outside and into the biting wind. He got out, helped Ella and Katie inside, then got in around the other side. Once they were all settled, he jiggled Rex's reins, and Rex took off at a happy trot.

Ella was seated right next to Loyal, and Katie noticed that she cuddled awfully close, like she was half stuck to his side. But after a few minutes, Loyal asked about their trip to the library.

Katie couldn't help but share her dilemma.

Loyal nodded. "That is too bad. I wonder why Jayne doesn't feel up to the project? It doesn't sound like that difficult of an undertaking. And it would be fun to see a big crowd out in the middle of our town on Christmas Eve, gathered around a living crèche."

"I think she's unhappy," Ella murmured. After a quick glance in Katie's direction, she added, "I saw the cover of the book Jayne was reading when we approached. It was titled *Finding Mr. Right.*"

Loyal laughed. "Maybe she's simply reading a romance."

"No, I've shelved that book. It's a self-help book for people who can't seem to get lucky in love."

"Like us?"

Katie inwardly groaned at the sweet puppy-dog looks they were giving each other.

But suddenly, it all made sense. A year ago, her uncle John had stopped dating Miss Donovan because he'd fallen in love with Mary Zehr. Ever since, Miss D. had seemed kind of blue.

Maybe Miss Donovan was lonely?

"We need to find Miss D. her own man," Katie decided. All before she'd realized that she'd spoken aloud.

"Katie, don't you dare start matchmaking," Loyal warned.

"But this is important. Miss D. needs to be happy, too. And if she was happy and in love, then I'm sure she'd feel more like helping with me the nativity."

Her brother groaned. "Katie, life isn't all about what you want."

"Oh, I know that. But even you can see that you two are happier together than you were alone. Miss D. would be happier with someone, too."

"Yes, but—"

"Lots of people come into the library, Loyal," she added in a rush as Rex clip-clopped toward home. "All we need to do is find one man who strikes her fancy."

"Strikes her fancy?" Ella echoed as she adjusted her eyeglasses a bit. "Oh, Katie. Falling in love isn't that easy."

"But God can help, and with Him, all things are possible. At least, that's what Mamm always says." When Loyal guided Rex to a stop at a red light, she paused for emphasis, because she knew that to be true. "Right?"

After a long moment, Ella slipped her arm around Katie's shoulders and squeezed gently. "Yes, dear. With God all things are possible, indeed."

As Loyal clicked the reins, and Rex started forward, Katie smiled. She was going to talk to God about the whole thing, and then, for sure, it was going to happen. Miss Donovan was going to find love and they were going to have a *wonderful-gut* Christmas nativity.

Just in time for Christmas.

Chapter Two

· · · · · · · · ·

AT A QUARTER to eight, Jayne Donovan began watching the clock in earnest. In fifteen minutes, she could shut down the computer, turn off the lights, and lock the door. In fifteen minutes, her terrible, no good, very bad day would be over.

She smiled at her private reference to the popular children's book. Before Ella, she'd never paid much attention to children's picture books. But now that Ella had been reading to the preschoolers for almost a year, Jayne realized she'd become as much a fan of children's literature as most of the four-year-olds in the area. There was something about Ella Weaver, and the stories she read, that was simply infectious.

It was really too bad that Ella was related to John Weaver, the Man She Hoped to Never See Again.

Which, of course, was a pipe dream. Jacob's Crossing was a small town, and John was Ella's husband's uncle. And one of Miss Katie Weaver's favorite people. And since Katie was one of Jayne's favorite children . . . well, it seemed they were destined to run into each other. Constantly.

The door burst open with a *whoosh*. "How soon do you close?" a man called out.

Jayne didn't recognize him. "Um, ten minutes," she said, feeling the hair on the back of her neck rise. "May I help you find something?"

"Yeah," he said, striding toward her in dark jeans, heavy work boots, a black ski jacket, and a determined expression. "I need a couple of mysteries by Lee Child. And a cookbook." Eyes the color of freshly brewed Starbucks looked at her directly. "Can you help me?"

"Of course." She was still attempting to quell her nerves when she noticed that his jacket had an insignia of the Jacob's Crossing Sheriff's Department. "You're a cop," she exclaimed.

He nodded. "Yeah." Still gazing at her in that direct way of his, he added, "Is that a problem?"

She decided to be honest. "Not at all. It just means you're not a psycho killer."

That drew him to a stop, and made a wry expression appear on his face. "You get a lot of those around here?"

"Of course not. It's just dark . . . and late. I guess my imagination got the best of me."

A reluctant smile lit his face. "I can see how that could happen, being surrounded by all these books."

Finally walking around from the safety of the circulation table, she smiled. "Is there a certain Lee Child title you're looking for? I can go get it while you look at the cookbooks."

"You always this helpful?"

"Only to cops and deputies," she quipped. Unable to help herself, she said, "My dad was a cop."

"Retired?"

"Yep. He put in twenty-five years with the Cleveland Police Department."

"I just moved here from Kentucky. A little town right outside of Paducah."

"Bit of a change from northern Ohio, I think."

"I'll say. The guys have been giving me a lot of grief about what I think is a lot of snow."

"We get that lake effect snow, what with Lake Erie being so close and all," she began before cutting herself off. "I'm sorry, I bet you've heard that one a lot."

"It's still true, though," he said wryly. "It's taken some getting used to, but I'm getting the hang of it." After glancing at the clock again, he said, "Either *Tripwire* or *Running Blind*."

"What? Oh, right. And let me take you to the cookbooks."

Fighting off a sudden blushing problem, she led him through the stacks to the back wall. "Here they are. I'll be right back."

"Thanks, Miss . . ."

"Jayne," she supplied. "Please, just call me Jayne." Surprising herself. Rarely did she give her first name. Rarely did anyone ever ask it.

"All right. Thanks, Jayne."

She skittered away before she did something dumb, and trotted to the fiction books. Glad for once that the fiction titles were shelved on the other side of the library, Jayne took a deep breath.

The man was in luck. She pulled both of the volumes. For a moment, she'd been tempted to hand him the books, just like an eager admirer, but she stopped herself in time. He'd come for books, not to be followed. So she forced herself to stand back at the circulation desk and wait.

A few minutes later, he strode out of the stacks, his hands full. When he saw her, he grinned. "Any luck?"

"I found both the titles, and it looks like you found what you were looking for, too."

"I did." His smile was suddenly boyish.

Her heart thumped a little faster. She struggled to keep her features neutral. No way did she want him to be aware of how he affected her!

"I don't believe you have a library card, do you?"

"No, ma'am."

She glanced at the time. "If you wouldn't mind just telling me your basic information, I'll enter it right into the system."

"No problem."

"Name?"

"Connor Fields."

"Address?"

"83 Wentworth Circle. Jacob's Crossing."

She stilled.

"What's wrong?"

"Nothing. It's just that you live on my street."

He smiled. "Who would have guessed?"

She smiled right back, got his phone number, then quickly scanned his books, noticing that the cookbooks were for Thai food. "That's pretty adventurous cooking for around here."

"I'm an adventurous guy."

She laughed as she handed him the books. "Have a good night, Deputy Fields."

"You too, Jayne."

He'd just grabbed his books when they heard a loud thump followed by a shrill scream.

It sounded like someone had just been attacked outside her door.

Her heart started beating faster and she grasped the edge of the circulation desk for support. "Connor?"

His expression had gone from relaxed and warm to all business in the space of a heartbeat. "Stay here for a sec, Jayne," he said over his shoulder as he strode toward the door. "Let me see what happened."

She stood where she was for a minute, but then curiosity got the best of her. She walked toward the door and practically pressed her nose to the cold glass windows that made up the middle of each door. This was her library, and she wanted to see what was happening, even if she didn't go outside.

At first she only saw Connor speaking with a man who looked about eighteen or nineteen. She waited and watched, trying to connect the screech she'd heard with the young man. Craning her neck, she tried to see more of the area around Connor.

Then she froze.

A woman about seventy years old was lying on the ground, right in front of the nativity. After saying something more to the man, Connor knelt beside her.

Jayne strained her eyes, doing her best to see through the

shadows cast by the front entryway's lights. Now she saw Connor was speaking on a cell phone. He had a strange expression on his face.

A trickle of fear knotted her insides. Whatever had happened hadn't been good.

Well, it certainly seemed that her no good, very bad day wasn't over yet.

Something very bad had just happened, and it had taken place practically on her front doorstep.

Chapter Three

· · · · · · · · · ·

JAYNE STOOD AT the door, her hand hovering over the handle as she debated whether to heed Connor's warnings or offer assistance.

Duty, and the sense that she needed to follow her heart led her outside. As she stepped out into the dark night, a burst of cold wind nearly forced her to turn around. The temperature had certainly dropped to the freezing mark and she hadn't even thought to grab her wool coat. Pushing aside her discomfort, she carefully tiptoed through the snow to Connor and the injured woman.

The man she'd first seen Connor talking to was nowhere in sight.

When Connor looked up, he raised a brow, but he didn't seem too upset. "Couldn't stay away?"

"I, uh, thought I might be able to help," she said. Crouching down into the snow, she looked at the lady, who seemed to be a little out of it. "Hi. I'm Jayne Donovan. The librarian."

Slowly, the lady looked her way. "So?" she said groggily.

Stung, Jayne rocked back on her heels. "Um, I thought you might need some help? Would you like to come inside the library and get warm?"

"We've got an ambulance coming," Connor said. "She's got a pretty good knot on her head."

"What happened?"

Before Connor could answer, the woman opened her eyes again. "I was attacked."

"Oh my goodness." Just as Jayne was about to ask another question, Connor shook his head slightly. Warning her without words to stop her questions.

Jayne nodded, and kept her own expression concerned. "I hope you aren't hurt too badly."

"I hope so, too," Connor said. "Luckily, the ambulance should be here in another minute or so."

Just as Connor stood up and pulled out his cell phone again, emergency sirens shrieked through the air.

Getting to her feet as well, Jayne watched an ambulance and two police cars park at the front of the lawn. "Help has arrived," she said with a tiny smile.

Jayne was about to offer to make phone calls to the woman's family when Connor glanced at her over his shoulder. "Jayne, why don't you go back inside? There's nothing you can do out here, plus I think we might be a little while."

"Oh, sure." She backed away, feeling curiously hurt that she'd just been dismissed. When she got back inside the library, she tried to think of something to do besides stand on the other side of the door and watch the men and women surround the lady and speak with Connor. But of course there was nothing that needed to be done. Not after eight at night.

Chilled, she rubbed her arms, then kept her arms crossed over her chest and continued to watch. For a moment, she considered calling someone, but realized that there really wasn't anyone in her life to call.

And how sad was that?

She'd been in Jacob's Crossing for just over a year. Soon after moving she met John Weaver. Though they'd only dated a brief amount of time, she'd really thought there was something special between them. When he broke things off in order to see someone else, she'd become so heartbroken that she'd practically shut herself off from everyone else.

Which had been really dumb.

No wonder she'd been reduced to reading self-help books in the stacks.

Seeing the older woman lying there on the ground all alone gave her a peek into her future that she didn't like. "Things need to change, Jayne," she told herself. "No way are you going to end up old and alone. You've got to make more of an effort to reach out to people."

As she watched a pair of EMTs help the injured woman onto a stretcher and two other uniformed men speak with Connor, Jayne felt tears spring to her eyes.

She felt sorry for the woman, out at night all by herself.

But Jayne realized she was also frightened. Had the woman been attacked on purpose? If Connor hadn't arrived and kept her occupied, could *she* have been the woman getting loaded on the stretcher?

Jayne winced as the sirens rang out and the ambulance turned around and sped down the street, one of the police cars on its tail. Slowly, she went back to the circulation desk and sat down in the comfortable chair behind it.

Quickly, she closed her eyes and said a prayer for the woman, and for the drivers and doctors and other medical personnel.

Even Connor.

Connor! Funny how now she was thinking of him on a first name basis.

With a *whoosh*, the glass door opened and Connor stepped in, followed closely by two other officers.

"How is she?" Jayne asked.

Connor exchanged a wry glance with the other two men. "I think she's going to be all right," he said cryptically. "It seems Mrs. Jensen was walking past the nativity when she was grabbed on the lawn, then fell."

Jayne felt a shiver flow through her. "That's awful!"

"It is, but I'm not exactly sure what actually happened. The man I was talking to? He seems to think he saw her slip and fall against the side of the wooden crèche. Or maybe a rock or something."

"There are some fairly big rocks around there. It was one of the reasons I put the display where I did. Most people go out of their way to avoid them." Then she recalled what the woman had said. "But she said she had been attacked."

"Yeah." Another man pulled at the collar of his shirt, like

it had suddenly become too tight. "She might have . . . or she might have made up her story when she got caught."

"Got caught doing what?"

"Trying to steal a figurine, to be exact," Connor said with a smile. "We saw quite a few tracks around the figures, and something that certainly looks like skid marks from something being pulled away."

"So, we're missing one of the pieces?"

"I'm afraid, so." He glanced at the other man before meeting her gaze. "Two other figures were toppled over when we got there. Mrs. Jensen could have fallen while trying to take yet another figure and tripped or something."

Jayne couldn't believe that anyone would want a piece of her very old nativity set. "Oh my goodness. How does something like that happen?"

He looked at the other two officers again. "I don't know, but I'm a little irritated. She wants to file a report. Which means I'm going to have to at least pretend I believe her and look around here a little bit closer. Not the way I wanted to spend my Friday night."

"I wonder why anyone would want one of our old figures?" she mused, mainly to herself.

Connor shrugged. "I've given up trying to figure out why folks do things. One of us will go to the hospital when we're done here and get a better statement. If she was hurt by a mugger, that's a pretty serious crime and we need to get some more information. But if she was trying to steal from you?"

"We'll have to investigate things along a different avenue," another man muttered.

"Well, this is shocking. And at Christmas, too." She flinched when she noticed all three men looking at her in amusement. "What's so funny?"

"It's odd, but this *is* Jacob's Crossing, Miss," the first man said. "Strange things have been known to happen on occasion."

"My name is Miss Donovan, Jayne Donovan," she supplied.

"Jayne, please meet Deputy Gomez and Sheriff Jackson. They're with Jacob's Crossing Sheriff's Department, too."

Too rattled to say much, she nodded a greeting.

He seemed to notice. With a gentle grip on her arm, he led her to one of the big comfy couches near the children's area. "You better sit down."

Sheriff Jackson pulled out a notebook. "Miss Donovan, I need to ask you some questions."

"I understand."

"So, have you seen Mrs. Jensen here before?"

Jayne tried to recall, but at the moment she was too shaken up to trust her memory. "Maybe. She kind of looks like one of the ladies who always come in for the new mysteries, but I can't really be sure."

"Do you talk to the patrons much?"

"Some. Those who ask for help." Thinking of her busy days, she struggled to explain. "Even if I have chatted with her and checked her out, we have a fairly large membership. She could be any number of women."

Her stomach dropped as the three men exchanged glances and Sheriff Jackson wrote down notes in his notebook.

"Have you ever seen anyone lurking around the building at night?"

"Like a man? Like a mugger?" She was starting to get alarmed again. "But . . . I thought you thought she might have been out stealing my nativity."

"She might have . . . but we just want to make sure we've followed every lead. So . . . have you seen anyone suspicious around lately?"

"No. But I don't leave by the front door, I go out through the back."

The questions continued. Some felt like they were the same exact ones, phrased and rephrased over and over. With each one, her nerves became more frazzled.

Finally, she said, "Should I be worried?"

"Jayne, I can't promise anything," Connor said. "But I think you should definitely keep your eyes open. You never know what could happen."

"But it's almost Christmas."

"Crazy things happen at Christmas, ma'am," Deputy Gomez said as he zipped up his jacket. With an exaggerated shiver, he said, "Lots of crazy things."

The two men left soon after, leaving her alone with Connor again.

"How about I walk you to your car, and then follow you home?"

"There's no reason to do that. I'm okay." Of course, she wasn't, but he didn't need to know that.

"Let me do this. Remember, I live on your street, so it's not like it's out of my way. Besides, you're rattled."

She couldn't deny that. "I am pretty shaken up, but I'll be fine." Eventually. When the shivers running up and down her spine subsided a bit.

Sympathy entered his eyes. "I'm sorry, I should have told you to call a friend or your boyfriend."

"I, um, don't have a boyfriend," she blurted before she thought to keep that little tidbit to herself. Before he could ask more questions that would lead her to admit just how empty she felt at the moment, she pasted on a smile. "Look, I'm going to be okay. You certainly don't have to follow me home. But don't forget your books."

Looking at his neat stack of books on the counter, he rubbed the back of his neck. "Boy, so much has happened, I almost forgot why I came in here."

"You'll remember when you're knee-deep in one of those thrillers. Enjoy your evening, Connor. I'll go ahead and lock up."

"I think I'll stay and walk you out."

"Sure?"

"Positive." He stood still while she bolted the locks on the front doors, made sure the desk drawers were locked, then paused at the door to the offices.

"The back door is this way," she said.

"Lead on."

Walking down the narrow hall with him felt strangely intimate. And when she stepped through the back door, waited for him, and then locked the door behind him, she felt even more aware of an unspoken familiarity.

He had her pause as he walked around her car, then nodded, signaling for her to get in.

Then suddenly, he was sitting beside her, and the cold, dark car was filled with his scent.

"My vehicle's on the street."

"Oh. Sure."

In no time at all, she was at his truck.

"Wait a sec and I'll follow you home," he said before exiting the car, slamming the door shut.

She waited, and felt his reassuring presence the whole drive home. When he pulled into her driveway behind her, he left his truck running as he walked to her window. "Are you sure that you're going to be okay?"

"Positive," she said, echoing what he'd said earlier. Jayne almost smiled, trying her best to look calmer than she felt.

"All right, goodbye then."

"Thanks, Connor. And, uh, Connor? Hope you enjoy the books."

He laughed. "Thanks. Night, Jayne. See you soon."

She only hoped that was a promise of good things to come . . . not a warning that things could soon be getting much worse. And maybe even more dangerous.

Chapter Four

·········

"KATIE WEAVER, CARE to tell me why you are sitting in bed, reading the Bible?" her mother asked when she entered her bedroom long after Katie was supposed to be asleep.

Katie gulped. Katie knew all too well that her mother only said her first and last name when she was upset with her.

Which happened to be fairly often.

Hands on her hips, her mother raised a brow. "Katie?"

"Yes, Mamm." Shoving the big, heavy book off her lap, Katie bit her lip. "I've got a *gut* reason. I mean, I do. Kind of," she mumbled. Raising her chin, she prepared to get yet another talking to.

But instead of chastising her for being up so late, her mother sat on the side of her bed. "Care to tell me why you are reading your father's Bible?"

"I didn't hurt it. I was real careful."

"So I see." Lifting the special book off the mattress, her

mamm put it on the bedside table. "But I'm asking because I know we've given you some children's books filled with Bible stories. They would be much easier to read, Katie."

"You did, and I like them fine. But I'm looking for something mighty important."

Her mother blinked. "You are? And what that might be?"

"I want to know everyone who was in the stable with Jesus."

"In Bethlehem when He was born?"

"Uh huh." She braced herself for another round of questions.

But instead of asking her why she was so interested, her mother retrieved the book and set it in her lap. Biting her lip, she flipped the thin, fragile pages to the Book of Luke. Then pointed to the second chapter. "It says here Mary and Joseph were in a stable. And an angel comes to visit the shepherds."

"Is there a donkey? What about a cow? And does it talk about sheep? Were there sheep?"

"Well, the shepherds were in the field. One can only assume they had sheep. But as for what animals were there in the stable . . ." she said slowly. "I have to say I'm not rightly sure." After skimming the text again, she leaned back against the headboard. "Katie, why are you so interested?"

"Because there's a nativity in front of the library, Mamm."

"Ah, yes. Ella did mention that you were interested in finding real people to fill the spots."

Glad that her mother was finally catching on, Katie nodded. "For Christmas Eve."

"Katie, we Amish don't usually honor nativities. You

know this, right? That's why we don't have one in our *haus*. All we really need is this book," she said, pointing to the Bible.

"I know . . . but I can't help it, Mamm. I like the nativity at the library. I like it a lot, and I want to make it pretty."

After a moment, her mother sighed. "I suppose I can't fault you for that. A beautiful nativity is, indeed, a wonderful sight to behold."

Her mother's expression softened for a moment, but then she closed the Bible once again and set it on the table. And looked at her sternly. "Ella also happened to mention that Miss Donovan wasn't interested in your plans."

"That's only because Miss D. is depressed about her love life."

Her mother closed her eyes, just the way she did when a headache was coming on. "Miss Donovan's personal life isn't any of your business."

"Don't worry, Mamm. We're going to fix her love life. Then she'll be able to think about other things."

Her mother's eyebrows rose. "We?"

Uh oh. She'd said too much. "Um, Ella and me?" Katie said weakly.

"Katie Weaver—"

"All right," she interrupted quickly, before another lecture came on. "Ella isn't too excited about that. It's just me who is." Glancing at the Bible on the table, she slumped. "But I can do it. Miss Donovan just needs to find someone who likes books. And who likes her, too, I suppose."

For a moment, her mother looked like she'd swallowed a bad-tasting pill. Then she exhaled with a *whoosh*. "Katie, if

I've said it once, I've said it a thousand times. You are twice as much work as your three older brothers combined."

That wasn't good. At all. "Mamm, I don't mean to be so much work."

"But you are, child. I don't think I had any gray hair before you arrived. Now look at me!"

Reluctantly, Katie looked at her mother's neatly pinned hair under her white *kapp*. Thick gray strands now kept company with her dark brown hair. Katie didn't think the gray strands looked bad, but she didn't think she should say that.

Her mother glowered as she held up one finger and waved it like a stick. "You may *not* start meddling in the librarian's love life. And you must learn to listen to people. If they say they're not interested in something, that means they aren't. It isn't an invitation to brush over their objections."

Getting to her feet, her mother picked up the Bible and held it close to her chest. "Do you understand?"

Oh, she understood, but she didn't agree. "Mamm, this is real important."

"It is not your concern."

Her mother's tone was clipped now—a sure sign that she was losing her patience. Usually, Katie would back off. But today she simply couldn't. "But Christmas is coming."

"It will still come without your interference, Katie." Turning toward the door, she added, "If you have so much extra time, I think you'd best get up early in the morning and help me in the kitchen. We've got cookies to bake and quilted potholders to make."

"I will," she said quickly, letting all her worries about Miss

D. fade. She loved helping her mother bake Christmas cookies. "I'll help you in the morning, Mamm."

Inch by inch, her mother's frown lines smoothed. "*Gut*. I love you, Katie. Now, close your eyes and go to sleep."

When she was alone again, Katie sighed. Her mother was right. She really didn't have much say in other people's business. Even her brothers had gotten married without much of her help. And though Loyal and Calvin had fallen in love fairly fast . . . Graham sure hadn't. Everyone in the family had known he and Mattie were meant to be married way before they did. After all, when Mattie had been fighting cancer, her brother Graham would hardly leave her side. Now Mattie was healthy and they were happily married.

How in the world was she going to find the librarian someone to love in just a week?

As she pulled her thick quilt over her shoulders, she snuggled down deeper into the feather bed. Wiggled her toes against the flannel sheets. Yawned.

Then closed her eyes and prayed to the only one who could help Miss D. "Jesus, I know you're getting ready to celebrate your birthday and all . . . but if it ain't too much trouble, I really need some help. See, if Miss Donovan doesn't get happy soon, all of us in Jacob's Crossing are gonna have to look at that stupid plastic nativity until Christmas. And we both know that it ain't right. We need a real nativity, with real people and real animals.

"And even though I'm not supposed to care about it, 'cause I'm Amish, I still do. I like seeing the shepherds and Mary and Joseph. And you as a little tiny baby, too. And I can't help but think that other people in Jacob's Crossing feel the same way. Sometimes seeing things up close and in person is the only way everyone can really believe."

Then, because there really didn't seem to be any more to say, Katie closed her eyes and went to sleep. It was in God's hands now.

Chapter Five

· · · · · · · · ·

THE NEXT DAY, after completing the last of the report, Connor reread it and frowned. The other deputy on duty, Trey Gomez, noticed.

"What's wrong?"

"I keep reading and rereading this report but I think I'm missing something. It's like something obvious is staring right at me, but I keep overlooking it." Glancing at Trey, he said, "Don't tell me you think I'm crazy."

"I won't. You've got to trust your instincts every time. They've sure saved me enough."

"Yeah. Me too."

Swiveling his chair to the side, Connor glanced at Trey. "So, no one has reported any other muggings during the last few weeks?"

"Not a one." Eyes lighting with humor, Trey said, "There hasn't been an outbreak of nativity burglaries, either."

"I can't even believe we're talking about a stolen wise man and a mugging in the same sentence." Jayne had called this morning and confirmed that one of her wise men was in fact missing.

"It's not that odd. This is Jacob's Crossing, not Detroit, Connor. Our crime looks a little different. A year ago, one Amish woman kidnapped another and took off with her in a buggy."

He dropped his ballpoint pen. "Did you say kidnapped?"

"You know I did." Trey shook his head. "People reported that she had a lot of emotional problems. Anyway, they ended up crashing, and the kidnapper died." Crossing one foot on the opposite knee, he continued. "It was a real tragedy. I'm only telling you this so you'll understand that crazy things can happen around here."

Connor rubbed the back of his neck. "I guess you're right."

Trey glanced at the mess of papers littering his desk, picked up a phone message, and winced. "Plus, Christmas makes people do strange things, too. All that happiness blaring on the television and radio can really make a lot of folks depressed."

"It was that way in Kentucky, too. It's probably that way everywhere."

Trey turned back to his computer. Glancing at his report, Connor located her name. "Mrs. Jensen is lucky she didn't sustain anything worse than a bad headache and a couple of stitches."

"She is lucky, though I can't help but wonder why she was even out so late last night."

Connor glanced at him in surprise. "It was eight on a Friday night, not midnight."

"I hear you, but her neighbors say she usually doesn't venture out after dinner." Trey scanned his notes again. "Actually, the neighbors say she rarely ventures out at all. And when she does, it's only to go to the library or to buy something."

"Maybe she simply wanted a book to read. I mean, that's why I was at the library last night." Experience had taught him that sometimes the simplest answer was the right answer.

Thinking about his quest last night made him think about Jayne. Even though he'd dropped her off at her house last night, he was anxious to see her again. "You know, I think I'm going to go back over to the library and look around. We could have missed something in the dark."

Trey looked at him for a moment, then shrugged. "Sounds good. Let me turn this report in, then I'll go with you."

"I'd rather go over there on my own."

"Why?"

"Oh, you've got other stuff to do. No need to worry about the library."

"So? We've always got tons of stuff to do." Trey's eyes narrowed. "Come on, 'fess up. What's the rest of your reason?"

"I'm kind of interested in the librarian."

Trey grinned. "I wondered if you were going to mention the beautiful Miss Jayne Donovan. So, got a crush on the librarian, huh?"

It was embarrassing to get teased about a lady he had hardly talked to, let alone worked up the nerve to ask out. "She's a nice woman."

"And pretty."

"We clicked."

"I'll just bet you did." Trey whistled low. "Maybe you're hoping for a little private investigating?"

"Shut up," he called out over his shoulder before his buddy started making even more cracks. "I only want to see her again. Make sure she's all right. She was a little shaken up last night."

Trey's grin only widened. "Let me know if you need help consoling her."

"I won't. And you shouldn't even be noticing her. You're married."

"I'm very married, and very happily married, too. But I'm not blind," Trey retorted. "Besides, you're always so calm, cool, and collected, I can't resist giving you a hard time."

"Happy to oblige," he said sarcastically.

He left the room with Trey's laughter ringing in his ears.

Connor figured he deserved the ribbing. Ever since he'd arrived in Jacob's Crossing, he hadn't done much besides work. And he'd been so burned by his old job and breakup with his girlfriend that he tended to act as if any woman was a potential shark.

Now, all of a sudden, he wanted to see more of the pretty brunette who seemed just as alone in her own way as he felt.

When he drove into the parking lot of the Jacob's Crossing Library, he noticed three buggies parked off to the side, their horses hitched but looking pleased enough to be munching on the winter grass sprouting out of the snow.

He nodded to an Amish man walking out of the library as he entered.

And then he felt as if he'd entered a far different world.

Unlike the quiet serenity of the previous evening, the library was brightly lit, and practically buzzing with the excited chatter of small children. One glance showed him the reason—it was story time.

Drawn by the scene, he stepped a little closer. To his surprise, an Amish woman in a crisp white *kapp* was reading a story in front of about twenty children. She had brown hair, glasses, and was obviously very pregnant. She wasn't beautiful as Jayne was, but there was something beautiful about her, he decided. Lovely.

Maybe it was her voice? Perhaps it was her obvious enthusiasm for the book she was reading. In spite of himself, he leaned against the wall and listened in to the Christmas story she was reading—something about a donkey.

"Is anything wrong?" a sweet, feminine voice murmured over his shoulder.

Startled, he turned to Jayne. "No. I came in here to talk to you, but I guess I got caught up in the story." He ran a hand through his hair. "Sorry, I don't know what happened. I can't recall the last time I listened to someone read a book aloud."

"Ella has that way about her," Jayne whispered with a smile as she motioned him farther away from the preschoolers. "I can't tell you the number of times I've stopped working and joined the kids for story time. There's something about Ella that's mesmerizing."

Connor liked that description. "I didn't know Amish women worked in libraries."

"I don't know if they do, as a norm, but it's been a perfect fit for Ella. Everyone loves her, and from a business standpoint, she's brought up our circulation numbers by twenty percent." She paused, nibbled her lip. "But I'm guessing you didn't stop by to talk about Ella, or her popular story time."

"I stopped by because I wanted to check on you. I know you were a little rattled last night. Are you okay?"

After glancing around to make sure nobody could overhear, she nodded. "I'm okay, but I have to admit I really was pretty shaken up. Seeing that woman collapse like that, being questioned by the sheriff . . . nothing like that's ever happened to me before."

"That's a good thing." He had the strangest urge to reach out to her. To wrap an arm around her shoulders and assure her that everything was going to be okay.

"So, how is Mrs. Jensen? Was she hurt badly?"

"She's got a few stitches, a lump on the back of her head, and a minor concussion, but she's going to be all right. She's home now, safe and sound."

"I don't suppose she knows who attacked her?"

He shook his head. "We'll keep looking, though. And I'm going to stop by to see her this afternoon. She might remember more now that she's recovered a bit." And maybe she'd also let him know why she had been wandering outside unusually late, for her at least.

"Let me know if she needs something. I could bring her soup or a pie."

"You'd do that?"

"She was hurt in front of my library, Deputy Fields."

"It's Connor, remember? And listen, what happened wasn't your fault, Jayne." Once again, he was tempted to offer her comfort. With effort, he kept his hands by his sides.

"I know . . ." She shrugged. "Even if it's not my fault, I'm still happy to bring her a meal. It's what folks here in Jacob's Crossing do for each other."

"I'll pass along your offer." Now that the business part of his visit was taken care of, he ached to make some dinner plans of his own. "So, I was wondering . . . what time do you get off work tonight?"

Her eyes widened. "Seven o'clock."

"Do you have plans afterward?"

"Um . . . no."

"How about we go grab a quick bite to eat then?"

Little by little, the worry in her eyes eased into something more playful. "Connor, are you asking me out or looking out for my welfare?"

Funny, he wasn't sure. Everything inside him wanted to make sure she was okay. But even stronger was his desire to get to know her better. "Both."

Her brows rose. "Both?"

He grinned. "That's not a bad thing, Jayne."

"No . . . no, I suppose it's not." She looked to add more when a little Amish girl approached, all bright blue eyes and smiles. "Hello, Katie Weaver."

"Hi, Miss Donovan." She looked at him curiously.

And to his surprise, Jayne's smile grew wider. "Deputy Fields, please meet my special friend, Katie Weaver."

He inclined his head. "Hi, Katie."

Eyes wide, she looked him over from head to toe. "Are you a policeman?"

"I am," he said, not bothering to clarify that he was a deputy in the sheriff's department.

"Oh, good."

"Why is that good?" Jayne asked.

Katie's eyes widened. "Miss D., didn't you notice what happened with the nativity?"

Jayne shared a worried look with him. For some reason, it felt as if all of his senses were completely attuned to hers. With effort, he tried to keep his response tempered. "What's wrong?"

"Mary's missing, and so is one of the kings!"

"Two pieces?" Jayne asked, her voice slightly squeaky.

Connor shook his head. "No, we're only missing one figure, and it was a wise man."

"*Nee.* Two are gone!"

Jayne knelt on one knee so that she was eye level with the little girl. "Katie, there was an accident here last night. Maybe Mary got knocked over."

"I don't think so. My brother Calvin and I were just standing in front of it, looking. Jesus's mom is gone." Looking more disturbed by the second, Katie frowned. "This ain't *gut*, Miss D. First we had an old, broken-down nativity, and now two of the pieces are gone. Christmas is going to be ruined."

"Connor, could you help us some more?" Jayne gazed up at him in that way that already made him want to promise her the world.

Even if he hadn't been a cop, he knew he would never want to refuse that look. "I'll go out there right now."

"See?" Jayne said, patting the girl's shoulder. "Everything isn't ruined. Not yet, honey." To Connor, she said, "The nativity is pretty important to Katie."

"It's special to everyone in Jacob's Crossing," Katie said. "But we don't have a good one now. Not anymore." Katie's bottom lip trembled as her voice rose a bit. "Can you call it a nativity without Mary? Miss D., we have to fix it or Christmas is going to be really bad."

For once, Connor knew exactly what to say. When he was growing up, his church had had a plastic nativity, then had replaced it with children for one week in December. He'd been a shepherd, a wise man, and for one night, a very reluctant Joseph. His sister had been Mary, and he'd taken it as a personal affront that he'd had to stand with his sister for three hours.

Leaning down, he smiled encouragingly at Katie. "I'm afraid Katie here might be right. We've got a mystery to solve. Stealing nativity figures is a pretty rotten thing to do."

Katie's eyes widened. "You do understand."

"More than you might think," he said dryly. Standing up, he stepped away and motioned Jayne closer. "Since I'm going to be around here so much, and I'm taking a personal interest in your nativity, I really think you should go out with me tonight. Jayne, will you please have dinner with me?"

"I'd be happy to," she replied. Looking flustered. And pleased. And just the slightest bit apprehensive.

Now that he'd secured more time with Jayne, he turned to the girl. "I think I better go do some detective work. Katie, let's go out and look at the scene of the crime."

To his delight, she didn't hesitate. She merely started walking ahead. "Let's go through the side door. It's a lot quicker."

"I'm right behind you."

Hardly stopping, she slipped on her cloak and led him out the library's glass doors and down a snowy hill.

There at the foot of the hill lay the somewhat sorry-looking nativity. He had to admit that it certainly did look worse in the daylight. "This is an old set, don't you think?"

"*Jah.* Miss D. told me it's real old. Like from 2004."

He hid a smile as they followed the stepping stones to the sidewalk to the front. From their new angle, it was immediately apparent that there were now two empty spots where figures used to stand.

Katie folded her arms in front of her chest. "Mister, what are we gonna do?"

Connor loved how the little girl had firmly planted herself into the middle of the investigation. "We'll have to ask some questions." Actually, except for the knock Mrs. Jensen took to her head, it looked like a teenage prank to him. "I'll look around, see what I can find." Tromping to the crèche, he stepped around the figures, halfheartedly looking for any evidence of who might have been stealing the figures.

To his surprise, he found a mitten and an empty beer can.

Neither might have anything to do with the assault or the theft, but he showed them to Katie. "I found these two things."

"Do you know whose mitten that is?" she asked.

"Uh, no. But I'll put them in an evidence bag just in case something else comes up." Considering that just about every person in Jacob's Crossing owned a pair of mittens or gloves, and any number of people could have tossed an empty beer can, Connor knew he was only going through the motions of collecting evidence.

He was about to try to temper Katie's hopefulness when he noticed that they'd attracted a little crowd.

"What's going on, Deputy?" an older man said.

"I'm investigating a theft." He thought about adding that there was also a possible assault, but he didn't want to stir up a panic.

"Someone stole Mary and a wise man," Katie blurted.

"That's a pretty low thing to do," the man said.

"I think so, too." Katie's frown deepened. "Poor Mary,"

"Any idea who did it?" another woman asked.

"Nope," Connor replied. "But we'll keep an eye on it. We'll drive by every couple of hours."

A few of the women looked concerned. "But in the meantime, what is going to happen?" the same lady asked.

Connor shrugged. "I guess it will just have to be an incomplete nativity." Even as he said that, though, he felt a little deflated. These people were looking at him for answers and help, and so far, he had nothing to give them.

"I was kind of hoping we'd have a real nativity, with real people on Christmas Eve," Katie said.

When the group started chatting about that, Connor began to wish Jayne was there to help answer the questions. Since she was still inside, he figured she must have gotten busy with work of her own.

The ladies were still chatting. Then one called out, "You know what? My son David was Prince Charming in his school play. We still have the cape. He'd make a pretty good wise man. Maybe I'll have him come stand with the figures on Christmas Eve."

"If David's going to be there, I'm sure I could make my Kaitlin stand out here as Mary," another man said with a wry grin. "Maybe even bring my son Charlie in to be an extra shepherd." Somewhat wryly he added, "Couldn't hurt."

"They'd do that?" Katie asked.

"The kids are ten and eleven. They'll have a great time."

As the other folks laughed, Connor noticed that Katie Weaver brightened.   When she tugged on his jacket, he leaned down to listen.

"We have three real people! Christmas won't be ruined!"

"You're right. Christmas Eve is definitely looking better," he said with a smile.

In spite of everything else that was going on, Connor suddenly realized that in the middle of all the commotion, his mood had brightened a bit, too. He'd just helped make a little girl happier, and he just happened to have a date planned with Jayne Donovan, the prettiest librarian in town.

Things could be a whole lot worse.

Chapter Six

· · · · · · · · ·

AFTER SAYING GOODBYE to Katie and promising to be back at seven to pick Jayne up for dinner, Connor double-checked Mrs. Jensen's address, then walked to her house.

It was only a block away, which made her appearance at the library so close to closing make more sense. Perhaps she liked to walk at night? He'd known people to do stranger things!

Glancing around the area, he noticed that most of the homes were the same size and shape. He remembered reading about the Sears catalog homes of the forties. Thousands of people bought the house kits, and many of the durable, charming structures were still being lived in today. Most on this block were decorated for Christmas—wreaths decorated the doors, trees were adorned with lights. More than a few had an assortment of lawn decorations in their front yards.

Surrounding it all was a blanket of snow, making him feel

like he'd stepped into the middle of a snow globe or a Currier and Ives Christmas card. Taking a moment, he cleared his mind and let the beauty of the day and the wonder of the season grip his heart. Of late, he'd been so wrapped up in his recent move and his desire to make a good impression at work that he'd rarely taken the time to appreciate the magic of the Christmas season.

At last, he came to Mrs. Jensen's address. Slowing his pace, he gazed at the front lawn. In contrast to the other homes, hers looked like a Christmas warehouse had exploded on the front lawn. Everywhere he looked, he saw Santas and reindeer, elves and snowmen. Stopping at the entrance to her walkway, he looked at everything more closely. Despite the multitude, her Christmas decorations looked worn and disappointed, a bit grubby, and more than a little unkempt. In the midst of the plastic and wooden figures, old twigs and branches lay in stacks and piles.

To his surprise, there was no car in her driveway. He wasn't sure why he'd assumed her relatives or friends would be over. Maybe because back home in Kentucky his whole family would have camped out if his grandma had been in the hospital?

It made him sad to think Mrs. Jensen didn't have that same kind of support system.

As he walked toward her front door, he noticed that a sizable number of old newspapers were tossed in a pile to the left of a sad-looking giant toy soldier. A large wreath with molting red cardinals with black beady eyes watched him as he approached.

Hoping no rodent actually lived in the thing, he stuck his hand in the middle and knocked.

The door opened, and there stood Mrs. Jensen herself. "Yes?" she said, looking at him with a wary expression.

"I'm Deputy Fields, ma'am. We met last night?"

Cloudy blue eyes merely stared at him in confusion.

"I was at the library when you got attacked," he reminded her gently. "May I come in?"

"Why?"

To his surprise, instead of stepping backward, she stepped closer, and gripped the side of the door even harder, so it was impossible for him to peek inside.

Alarms started ringing in his head. He didn't need much more of a signal that something was going on. With effort, he kept his expression passive. "I have a couple of questions for you, Mrs. Jensen. Don't worry, it won't take long."

Lifting her free hand to her receding hairline, she glared. "I already told you people that I don't know who hit my head."

"I remember. But I have some other things to talk to you about." When she didn't budge, he tried to lighten things a bit. "This is kind of funny, but we're starting to think that maybe someone hit you when they were stealing part of the Christmas nativity that you were standing by."

Pure alarm flashed across her face before she seemed to firmly push it aside. "Why would you think that?"

"Several pieces are missing." Since she still looked wary, he heaped on his old Kentucky charm. "So, may I come in and talk to you? It's kind of cold out here to be chatting, don't you think?"

His charm—or lack thereof—didn't work. "I don't let strange men in my house."

O-kay. "Did you happen to see anyone around you before you were hit?"

"No."

"No one at all?"

"No." She looked at him disdainfully. "Now I'm cold, and I have a headache. I have nothing more to say."

She closed the door before he had time to draw another breath.

Connor stepped back and started down her walkway, but this time, he stepped off her walkway and walked onto the grass, taking time to look around her property a little more carefully. Mrs. Jensen might simply be a grumpy old woman.

Or she might have another reason for not wanting him to come inside or for not answering his questions.

After a pause, instead of walking back to the street, he strode up her driveway, noticing that it didn't lead to a garage, just a fence with a ramshackle-looking gate.

He'd just bypassed Blitzen when he noticed a smooth track in the hard snow. Something had recently been dragged up that driveway and through the gate.

He wondered what it was.

Getting out his cell, he took a picture of the marks to show the sheriff. It probably wasn't enough to justify a search warrant, but it was definitely enough to make him to decide to keep an eye on one grumpy woman with a propensity to collect sad-looking Christmas decorations.

"KATIE, WE MUST be going home now," her *mamm* said with more than a touch of impatience. "We have much to do to get ready for Christmas."

As was often the case, her relatives had taken turns carting her around. She'd gone to work with Ella, now her mother was picking her up while Ella continued her job at the library.

But even though her mother was in a hurry, Katie couldn't seem to stop herself from trying to delay doing chores at home.

"Can we go to Onkle John's donut shop first?"

"Katie—"

"Please? I haven't seen him in weeks and weeks."

"We've all been so busy, I suppose it has been a while." After glancing at Katie again, her mamm sighed. "We'll stop by the shop, but just for a moment." After making sure her bright green wool mittens were securely on, her mother took her hand, and together they took a left turn out of the library.

Katie loved walking around Jacob's Crossing, and especially at Christmastime. Many of the shop owners had strung white lights around their trees and hedges and left the lights on both day and night. Lots of stores also played Christmas music, so it was possible to hear snippets of music wherever a person walked in town.

Of course, all the shops and buildings were decorated with red bows and green wreaths. In the middle of the town square, the mayor had set up a giant Christmas tree. Miss D. had told her that the firemen had used their giant ladders to string the lights. "I love it here," Katie exclaimed. Unable to help herself.

To her delight, her mother squeezed her hand. "I do, too, Katie. Everything looks *wunderbaar!*"

Before she knew it, they were standing in front of her uncle's donut and coffee shop, the Kaffi Haus. Her uncle John was her father's brother, and what was special about him was that he'd been raised Amish, had become on *Englisher* for twenty years, then returned to Jacob's Crossing just two years ago.

They'd all been glad for his company, especially her brothers. Uncle John had a matter-of-fact way about him that made him a good person to turn to for advice.

He'd also recently married Mary Zehr. She was Amish, too. Now Onkle John was Amish again, and a busy man, helping to raise Mary's son, Abel. Abel was fifteen and handsome. Katie secretly had a tiny crush on him, though she'd never let anyone know about that.

"Do you think Abel is here?" she asked her mother as they walked up the short walkway to the shop's front door, keeping their pace brisk on account of the cold wind.

"There's a *gut* chance he might be. He likes to work with John, I think."

"I hope he is," Katie blurted before she remembered that no one was supposed to know how much she liked him.

Her mother smiled but said nothing about that, thank goodness.

Katie was happy to see that Abel was there when they opened the front door to the Kaffi Haus. He was wiping down a counter and chatting with two Amish boys who were seated at the coffee bar in front of him.

He straightened when she and her mother came in, and smiled. "Hello, Aunt Mary. Hiya Katie."

She smiled right back. "Hi, Abel. Hi, Onkle John."

Her uncle strode forward and scooped her up and gave her a little twirl. "How's my best girl?"

She giggled. "Good. Can I have a donut?"

"Of course. That's why you came, ain't so?"

Her mother gazed at John with fondness in her eyes. "We also came to see you two."

"We're glad you did." As he walked back behind the counter, he said, "Now what would you like?"

"Do you have any custard filled?"

"Yep. I'll get you one. Now, what have you two been up to this morning?"

"We had story time at the library," Katie said as she climbed up on one of the bright red stools on the other side of the counter.

"If you've just left from the library, I'm surprised you don't have an armful of books."

"I've got some books at home that I forgot to bring back." After she took a seat next to the boys, she told him all about the nativity, the missing figures, and how three children were going to fill in for them for an hour or two on Christmas Eve.

While she talked, she heard her mother telling her uncle about the missing nativity pieces, too.

"You're staying busy. And the police are involved in such a thing?"

"I believe so. While Katie was listening to the story, some

other mothers filled me in. A woman was injured last night," her mother explained. "She even had to go to the hospital."

Abel looked at his friends and smirked. "I wonder why anyone really cares about some stolen plastic figures."

Immediately, Katie felt hurt. "They're special, Abel," she said. "Real special. And Mary is Jesus's *mamm*, you know."

He glanced at his friends again and bit his lip. "Lots of folks have plastic figurines like that. If one gets broken, you can get a new set at the store. You know that, right?"

"Of course I do," she mumbled around a bite of her treat. Her heart sank as she realized that Abel was kind of making fun of her.

"Then why are you making such a fuss?"

Against her will, tears started to form in her eyes. "I'm not—"

"That's enough, Abel," Uncle John said sternly. "Katie here has a point. It's a sad day when biblical figures are being stolen, and that's a fact."

Abel tucked his chin. "Yeah . . . I guess so."

Just then, her mother stepped up behind her and squeezed her shoulders lightly. "We need to pay and move on, child. We have Christmas cards to work on. And baking, too."

"No charge for one donut, Mary."

As she always did, her mother shook her head. "That's not what we said we'd do, John. I'm not going to take advantage of you." She put two dollars on the counter and then motioned Katie to come along. "Come over for supper soon, you two. And bring Mary."

"Will do." He winked at Katie. "I'll be on the lookout for wayward wise men, Katie."

"*Gut*," she said, with a tiny glare in Abel's direction, before rushing to catch up with her mother, who was already standing at the door.

Chapter Seven

· · · · · · · · · ·

WHEN ELLA GOT off work that afternoon, Mattie and Lucy, her two sisters-in-law, were waiting in Mattie's buggy to pick her up. "This is a surprise."

"But hopefully a *gut* one?" Mattie asked.

"Of course. What are you two doing here? I thought you both were working on your Christmas gifts." Though the Amish didn't usually exchange gifts, they each gave small homemade ones to their husbands and to their mother-in-law. And to Katie, of course.

But, like the English, their days kept getting the best of them and they were all hopelessly behind. Lucy in particular had said she wasn't going to leave her kitchen table until she finished the table runner she was stitching for her mother-in-law. Lucy had Timothy to take care of, and Ella could hardly imagine getting anything done with an eighteen-month-old demanding all your attention. Timothy was a sturdy handful.

"Mamm has Timmy and we needed a break," Mattie explained as she clicked the reins to guide her horse and buggy forward. "Plus, we were thinking about you. How are you feeling?"

"All right. Tired. You know how it goes, Lucy."

"Unlike you, I took lots of naps." After a pause, Lucy turned to look at her. "Do you think you're maybe doing too much?"

"Not at all. At least, I don't think so." Ella shifted uncomfortably in her seat, rubbing her back as she did so in the hopes that it would ease the cramp.

Lucy noticed. "Is your back hurting you worse today?"

Usually she would shake off her discomfort, but it was bothering her too much to ignore. "*Jah*. I still have three weeks to go, too." As she shifted again, she glared at her stomach. "I'm so big! Every time I'm sure I can't get any bigger, I do. I'm going to be as big as a house soon."

Mattie giggled. "I don't think quite that big."

"You still look pretty, Ella. Why, every time Loyal looks at you, it seems that his eyes get all soft and sweet."

"Loyal is a kind husband, for sure." Sometimes she couldn't believe she and Loyal were actually married. Though they'd known each other for years, they'd never been close. He, all blond good looks and charm, had been a favorite of most everyone. She, on the other hand, had preferred to remain hidden behind her glasses.

Ella had been sure she would spend most of her life watching him from afar. But now they were married, and living on the land she was born on. And she was expecting his child! Wonders never ceased.

"When do you stop working?" Lucy asked.

"This Friday. I don't work all that much, anyway. I'm down to fifteen hours a week. Mainly all Jayne lets me do now is read to the *kinner*."

They talked about all sorts of things on the way home. About their husbands and homes, about how big Timmy was getting. They talked about recipes they were trying out, and about life as newlyweds.

More than once, Lucy and Mattie shook their heads in wonder about the path the Lord had taken them on. Lucy would have never met Calvin if she hadn't come out to help her cousin Mattie go through chemotherapy treatments for breast cancer. Now, here they were, both cousins and in-laws ... and best friends with Ella, who had grown up next door to the Weaver boys, never imagining she might have the chance to join their busy family.

Though Mattie tried to get her to go home and rest, Ella insisted on going to Lucy's. She and Calvin lived with their husbands' mother, Mary. Mary was so easy to be around, Ella knew she'd feel better in no time. "I want to help make cookies."

"It's going to be noisy. Tim will be up and the men will be around, too. You should rest, Ella."

"I'll lie down on the couch if it gets to be too much. I promise."

"All right," Mattie said. "But if I start worrying about you, I'm going to tell Loyal."

"If you do, I'll remember that and be sure to treat you like a child when you're in the family way."

An hour later, Ella was wishing she'd heeded her girl-friends' warnings. She was tired, and her back hurt even more than before. Even worse was the fact that her babe had begun to be even more active, which filled her with both wonder and pain, and the skin of her stomach stretched even more.

She soon realized that lying down would only make her concentrate on her aches instead of allowing her rest. She stood up and stretched. "Mary, I'll roll out cookie dough, if you don't mind."

"I don't mind a bit. Maybe being on your feet might help ease your discomfort."

Blushing a bit, she asked, "Have I been that obvious?"

"Only to someone who's had four children."

Waddling closer, she murmured, "Did standing up on your feet help you?"

"Not really," her mother-in-law said with a grin. "When I was expecting Graham, I had Calvin and Loyal underfoot. All I ever wanted to do was sleep."

Ella shared a look with Mattie. "We're sure glad you suffered through with our husbands," she said with a laugh.

"Indeed," Mattie said.

"What about with me, Mamm?" Katie asked.

"For you, child, I think I was in such shock, I hardly ever felt uncomfortable! You were our unexpected gift from the *engels*." She smiled.

As the other women laughed, Ella competently rolled out the sugar dough. When the dough was smooth, she said, "Katie, where are the cookie cutters?"

"Here they are." She brought over a basket filled with

lovely copper and silver shapes. Stars and hearts and candy canes kept company with stockings, bells, and other Christmas shapes.

Ella picked up one and admired its copper gleam. "These are so lovely."

"Some were my *mommi*'s," Mary said. "They've been in the family for years. And, since you like to bake like I do, one day they'll be yours, I reckon."

Ella turned to notice Katie right at her elbow. "Did you like today's story?"

"Uh huh. That donkey was so silly! Your *boppli* is going to be the luckiest baby in the world, Ella."

"And why is that?"

" 'Cause you're going to read to it all the time. And you're the best reader."

"You're sweet to say that. Maybe when you're older, you can read your niece or nephew books, too."

"I'd like that."

As Ella continued to press the cookie cutters into the dough, then carefully set each piece of shaped dough onto a baking sheet, Katie piped up again, "Ella, what do you think is going to happen at the library?"

"Do you mean with Miss D.?"

"Uh huh. Do you think she's happier yet?"

Ella knew Jayne had a date with the handsome deputy that evening. But she wasn't sure if Jayne wanted that to be common knowledge. And if Ella told Katie, it was sure to practically announced from the rooftops! "I think she is happier."

"That's good." She handed Ella a bell-shaped cookie cutter. "But what is she going to do about all the nativity pieces?"

"I'm not sure about that, dear." Looking at the other women in the kitchen, Ella said, "Did you all hear about the terrible thing that happened last night? A woman was knocked down right outside the library while Jayne was inside."

"Is she all right?" Mattie asked.

"She's fine now, but she had to get several stitches. Luckily the deputy seems to be keeping a close eye on things."

"It's a shame such a thing happened. A little scary, too," Lucy said from the kitchen table, where she was feeding Timmy some of the applesauce they'd canned together in the fall.

"It is," Ella murmured, thinking about how scared she'd been when she'd been kidnapped by her supposedly "best" friend.

Mattie was heating up hot chocolate at the stove. "Jayne was unharmed, though, right?"

"Oh *jah*. Actually, that deputy was inside, checking out books, when it happened. He saved the day."

"That was a blessing," Mary said.

"Indeed." Picking up the rolling pin, Ella moved on to the gingerbread cookies and carefully rolled the gingerbread dough into a neat oval. "What was also a blessing was that Deputy Connor Fields is handsome. And single."

Katie picked out a star and carefully pressed it into the dough. "Why was that a blessing?"

Oh dear. So much for trying to keep Jayne's date a secret. "Because he and Miss Donovan are going out on a date."

Katie froze. "She's in love? Already?"

Mattie held up a hand. "Katie, what do you mean by *already*?"

"Miss D. is too worried about finding love to help with the Christmas nativity. But if she's in love already, then she'll be happier and be sure to help me out."

Her mother sighed. "Katie Weaver, if I've told you once, I've told you a hundred times. Your wishes and wants don't always come first."

"I know. But this is important."

Clicking her tongue, Ella said, "I think an attack outside the library is more important, dear," She chided.

"It is. But . . . now we've got a thief, too."

"Thief?" Mattie shook her head in amazement. "I wouldn't have guessed it, but things are mighty exciting at the library."

"That is true." Briefly, Ella told Mattie and her mother-in-law about the missing nativity figures and how some *English-ers* had volunteered to stand in for the figures for Christmas Eve.

"I wonder if Graham could help in some way," Mattie mused, just as he came into the kitchen.

"Any cookies ready to be eaten yet?"

Without a word, Mattie handed her husband a sour cream cutout fresh from the oven. After he bit into it and smiled, she said, "Graham, what do you think about you and Loyal going out to the library sometime Monday to work on the crèche? It could certainly use a fresh coat of paint."

"Ah, I've heard about your interest in the nativity set. Will this make you happy, Katie?"

Eyes wide, she nodded.

Graham smiled then, making everyone chuckle. "Then I guess I will do it."

Ella smiled around another cramp, rubbing her back as she did. She didn't want to create a fuss, but she was really starting to wonder if she and the baby were going to be able to hold out another three weeks. At the moment, it felt mighty unlikely.

Chapter Eight

· · · · · · · · ·

IT WAS TEN minutes past seven, and Jayne was beginning to feel like she'd been stood up. The feeling was completely ridiculous, of course. This date had been Connor's idea—he wouldn't have forgotten.

But she still felt nervous and on edge. Connor was the first man since John Weaver she'd felt any attraction to. She was learning her love life was definitely in God's hands. She never would have chosen an Amish man or a sheriff's deputy. She would have looked for someone a little more like herself—someone who enjoyed being around people, but was a little bookish, too. Someone who had a fairly quiet life—not one involving crime and danger.

The fact was, she liked the quiet. She liked feeling calm and safe and in control. She really didn't like how she'd been feeling lately.

Ever since the incident, she hadn't been able to shake the

sudden batch of nerves that now consumed her whenever she considered walking outside after dark. Where before, she'd thought nothing of running down the street to the deli before heading home, now she felt her palms get damp simply walking out to her Honda in the back parking lot.

Though she knew it was only her imagination, she kept thinking that she was being watched. Or followed.

She didn't think that was truly the case. What had happened was that she'd lost her confidence and trust. Both in herself and in her new town. All it had taken was one hour to shatter her faith that everyone in Jacob's Crossing was a prospective friend.

Now she looked at everyone with suspicion. Even at the grocery store, she'd gazed at the other people in line, wondering if one of the men was so desperate that he'd attacked an elderly woman in the front of the library.

And the shenanigans with the nativity bothered her, too. She'd become a librarian because she believed in her heart that a library could still be the focal point of a town. That it was one place where everyone was welcome, and where everyone could find something he was looking for.

Now, it seemed that she might have been the only person who truly believed that.

Why, if Katie Weaver wasn't so fixated on having a true nativity and if other people hadn't volunteered to step in and fill in the missing parts, Jayne knew she would have put the whole thing back into the storage unit. Actually, she was so rattled, she was tempted to take down her Christmas tree, box up her garland, throw away the wreath she'd bought for the front of her home, and hide out until January 2. Strange things were happening, and she didn't care for it one bit.

The front door blew open. She started in surprise.

And then felt immediately embarrassed. Because Jacob's Crossing's newest deputy had finally arrived.

"Sorry I'm late," he said with an attractive smile that looked as breezy as his slightly windblown hair.

"You came," she blurted.

His footsteps slowed as she watched him take in her firm grip on the countertop, her wary expression, and the faint sheen of perspiration that now dotted her upper lip.

"Well, yeah." Compassion entered his gaze. "Hey, are you okay? You look at little upset."

Grabbing a tissue, she turned her back and dabbed at her face. "I'm fine, just a little cold."

As he approached, she turned back around and tried to smile. Little by little, she became aware of the smell of soap and aftershave. How his hair was damp—he must have gone home to shower before meeting her. "I actually have a pretty good reason for being a few minutes late. I was so sweaty, I thought I'd better shower before getting within ten feet of you. Kind of as a matter of public service."

His comment made her smile. "It's been that kind of day?"

"Yep. Now, what's your story? Why are you looking so keyed up?"

"No matter how much I try, I can't shake the memory of Mrs. Jensen lying there on the ground. I'm starting to imagine that everyone in the town is a suspect," she said sheepishly. "I know that's not true. I'm just still a little on edge, I guess."

When he came to a stop, he was standing so close, she could see that there were fine lines around the corners of his eyes. And a faint scar next to his upper lip. Those marks added character, she thought.

"You don't have to apologize for being rattled. It *is* scary, having a crime take place right where you work. I know it's hard to deal with."

"I guess you've been through this before."

"Well, I've been around my fair share of criminals and victims, but I have to say I don't think being around crime gets any easier. And it doesn't mean I think your feelings are silly," he murmured.

As he continued to gaze at her, time seemed to slow. For a moment Jayne thought Connor was going to put his arm around her. "Besides, from what everyone has been telling me, there's not a lot of crime in Jacob's Crossing. What happened to Mrs. Jensen is pretty unusual."

Looking into his eyes, Jayne realized he was telling her the truth. "Thanks. I feel better already."

He looked pleased. But then a thread of doubt entered his gaze. He had one hand on the back of a chair, and it looked like he was gripping it fairly tightly. "Jayne, do you still want to go out to dinner with me?"

"I do."

"Great." He exhaled, and the muscles in his jaw relaxed, as if he'd been worried she'd changed her mind. "Why don't you lock up and then we'll walk to the restaurant."

"Walk? But it's snowing outside." And, of course, it was dark.

"We'll be okay. You've got on boots, right?"

"I do. But—"

"Come on." Reaching out a hand, he took hers and squeezed gently. "I thought you said all this snow didn't faze you in the slightest."

"I might have been exaggerating a bit." Besides, she really wasn't too eager to be out in the elements. Driving her Honda two miles home was quite a bit different from tromping around on icy sidewalks in the dark.

"Come on, then. Take a chance." He grinned, revealing a dimple. "It's a pretty night, Jayne."

It was the dimple that did it. Or maybe it was the way he'd phrased things—that taking a chance, walking by his side in the dark, bundling up in the snow, it was a little bit exciting.

A little bit like jumping off a cliff.

"All right." After grabbing her coat, hat, and purse, she locked the door, then took his arm as they stepped out onto the sidewalk. "You really are enjoying all this snow, aren't you?"

"Yep." He shrugged, looking slightly sheepish. "I can't help it. Until moving here, the most snow I'd ever been around had been a half inch in February . . . and it was half ice. This snow is really pretty. Especially at Christmas."

His enthusiasm made her want to push aside all her worries and fears. And realize that here at Christmastime, she really did have so much to be thankful for.

Gosh, when was the last time she'd taken the time to

count her blessings instead of concentrating on her faults? Or worrying about everything that had to get done?

It was too long for comfort.

"Watch out, it's slick here," he murmured, moving a little closer to her, sliding his hand from her elbow to her waist.

His touch was what she needed. It calmed her, made her believe that she was still attractive.

And it made her feel secure, too. Both from the elements and from anyone dangerous lurking about. She moved a little closer to him, taking comfort in his steadiness. As they walked, she heard the telltale noise of horses' hooves. Turning around, she watched two buggies slowly make their way down the road. One was a traditional black buggy with Plexiglas. The other was a courting buggy. Even in winter, the smaller, jauntier looking buggy had no covering. Inside were two Amish teens. Both were bundled up, with scarves and mittens and a thick blanket covering their laps. Both the boy and the girl wore bright smiles . . . and both seemed practically oblivious to the sweet picture they presented.

Yet Connor noticed. "That's nice. You're going to think I'm really crazy, but I think that looks like fun."

She shook her head. "I don't think you're crazy at all. I feel the same way."

They shared a smile. And little by little, Jayne's worries started to drift away. She was on the arm of a strong, brave policeman. He wasn't going to let anyone attack them.

She needed to remember that.

A mere five minutes later, they were in Bravo's, the town's finest restaurant. It was an Italian restaurant located in an old farmhouse that had been completely refurbished and re-modeled. Decorating the door was a fresh pine wreath and a swag of greenery. White lights decorated the roofline. Inside, there were more white lights and a fresh balsam smell that surely invited even the most stalwart Scrooge to celebrate the season. Bravo's was owned by another pair of recent trans-plants to the region, but had quickly become the restaurant of choice for many of Jacob's Crossing's inhabitants.

After hanging up their coats on the rack by the door, they walked to the hostess station. Jayne was soothed by the glow of candlelight and charmed by the many brass and pewter "trees" decorating the tables. On each tree hung two or three ornaments.

Floating through the air was an instrumental version of "O Come, All Ye Faithful." "It's beautiful in here," she said around a little gasp. "I heard it was."

He looked at her in surprise. "You haven't dined here before?"

"No." She wanted to say that it was the type of restaurant to visit on a date. But if she said that, she would give her loner status away. Which would be beyond embarrassing. After all, a girl had to have some secrets. "But I'm glad I'm here now."

As the hostess guided them to their table, a table only big enough for two directly in front of a stone fireplace, she thought she spied him smiling.

She hoped he was. Suddenly, she felt like she was glowing like a Christmas tree.

CONNOR WAS PRETTY sure that everything about Jayne Donovan was perfect. Her violet eyes were striking. He loved her short brown hair and the way the ends curled at the nape of her neck, emphasizing her pretty features. He admired her slim figure, how she was wearing an ivory turtleneck, brown wool slacks, and simple gold hoops in the ears. She looked classy and pretty. Perfect. But everything about her manner revealed that she didn't see herself that way. No, she seemed oblivious of her beauty and unsure of herself. Almost awkward.

Over the years, he had spent his days around many women in uniform. They were feminine, for sure. But the women he worked with were also some of the most confident people he knew. They had to be, working in a man's world. He'd admired them, for sure.

But he'd be lying to himself if he pretended he didn't know which type of lady he preferred. There was something about Jayne that melted his heart.

After they ordered, Jayne glanced his way. "Would you mind if I said grace real quick?"

"I would love it." And he did feel that way, he realized with some surprise. Everything about this evening was feeling like it was the start of something special. Being around Jayne, enjoying the quiet serenity of Jacob's Crossing . . . and remembering who had placed him there.

After a hesitant smile, Jayne closed her eyes and recited a quick, quiet prayer. When he said, "Amen" with her, their eyes met, and again, a sweet feeling of happiness and peace passed through him. Sure, his job was filled with uncertainty. Sure, he was in a strange place, and it was taking some time for him to feel like he fit in . . . but things were also very, very good.

At least they were at that moment.

Then, their meal arrived. As they savored each course, enjoying crisp Caesar salads and homemade Italian bread and pasta with red sauce, Connor discovered more and more things about Jayne. He shared some of his history, too . . . about how he put in four years in the marines before going to the police academy, then taking his first job near his hometown in Kentucky.

And, of course, they talked books. He revealed how he'd already read half of *Tripwire* and was anxious to continue the story before he went to sleep.

But all too soon, their tiramisu and coffees were done, it was almost ten, and it was becoming obvious that the staff at Bravo's were anxious for them to go on their way.

As they walked back to the library, their steps slowed. The Christmas lights on the surrounding buildings made him think of glowing fireflies, and the smell of snow and fresh pine felt invigorating.

He wasn't in any hurry to say goodbye to her, though he knew that he shouldn't push his luck and try to get her to hang out with him a little longer. Though, of course, where would they even go? Jacob's Crossing looked locked up tight. "I guess things close up here pretty early, even on a Saturday night," he commented.

"Yep. Especially in the winter, when it gets dark so early."

"Doesn't it cramp your style?" he teased. By now he knew she favored quiet evenings in front of the fire.

"Yeah, it really has forced me to cut back on my bar hopping," she quipped. "It's been a difficult adjustment, but I've done my best to make do."

"I'm doing my best as well," he joked. He was just about to walk her to the library's back parking lot, wondering if he should kiss her cheek or her lips good night—when she pointed to the nativity and gasped. "Darn it! Connor, another figure has been stolen."

Before he could caution her to be careful, she trotted to the snow-covered lawn and moaned.

He trekked through the snow, too, and looked at the lonely remaining figures. "Who was taken this time?"

"Another wise man. And a lamb! Oh, who on earth would take a plastic lamb?"

"I hope this set didn't mean a lot to you."

"I've had it for years, but no, it doesn't mean all that much to me. Katie Weaver, however, is going to be so upset. Now we'll need even more people to help out on Christmas Eve."

He loved how she cared about the little Amish girl's feelings. "Tell Katie I'll ask around. These pieces aren't that small. Someone has got to have seen a plastic wise man in the back of someone's car or truck. And any, uh, lambs."

"Thanks," she said. "I know it probably seems like nothing to you, but like I said, these thefts are starting to get me rattled."

"They'd rattle anyone." Giving in to temptation, he brushed a stray strand of hair behind her ear. "Listen, I promise we'll continue to keep a lookout. But in the meantime, there's nothing we can do about it tonight, Jayne. Let me get you home."

She stepped a little closer to him, seeming to find comfort in his touch.

He was happy to oblige, and wrapped an arm around her shoulders. "I promise, I'll keep hunting for the thief."

"Thanks." Looking at him through half-lidded eyes, she said, "Are you going to try to follow me home again?"

"Maybe." When he spied her look of dismay, he shifted around, so that he had both hands loosely linked behind her waist. "I mean, it depends."

"On what?"

She was standing so close, her chin tilted up at him. Her lips slightly parted.

"On whether I get a kiss good night, of course." He'd already decided kissing her cheek was for the birds.

"Kiss you? On our first date?" Her brows rose, but her eyes sparkled.

"It is technically our first date, but we've been through a lot lately," he said, doing his best to look put upon. "Dealing with stolen nativity figures isn't easy. I've been around the library a lot, too. And we did spend quite a bit of time here when I came in for cookbooks."

"That's when Mrs. Jensen was attacked and I got questioned!"

"It still counts, in dating terms."

Her lips curved up. "I suppose I should kiss you then. Just to make sure you stay around. All to keep Katie Weaver happy, of course."

"She'll be happy to hear that you're doing everything you possibly can to help. That's important," he murmured. Just as he pressed his lips to hers, right there on the library's front lawn.

He felt a little bad he didn't wait until they were standing somewhere more private. But sometimes a man could be patient for only so long— and he had been thinking about kissing her for the last two hours. That was long enough.

Because, of course, her kiss was just about the sweetest thing he could have imagined.

Chapter Nine

· · · · · · · · · ·

KATIE LOVED HER books. She loved tagging along with her older brothers and her new sisters when they ran errands. She loved making snowmen, and she loved how her uncle John almost always brought her two custard and chocolate donuts whenever he came to the house.

But she most certainly did not love the thief who kept stealing the nativity figures from the front of the library.

On Monday morning, as she was standing next to Graham and Loyal, she gazed in dismay at the sorry-looking nativity. All that was left was a grumpy-looking cow, a donkey missing one of its ears, one wise man, and a sad-looking Joseph. Oh, and a really run-down looking crèche. "Things are getting worse by the second," she stated.

Her brother Graham took off his hat and scratched his head. "It sure seems that way, Katie. I've never heard of a person taking biblical figures before. It sure don't seem right.

And taking a plastic lamb? That just seems dumb. I sure wouldn't want a lamb that looked like this."

"You should see the baby Jesus that Miss D. has waiting in her storage room!" Katie grumbled. "He doesn't look good at all. Kind of sickly, if you want to know the truth."

"Sickly, hmm?" Graham coughed, just like he was trying not to laugh. "Well, what I want to know is why would anyone want to steal the figures?"

"I have no idea. But the whys of it don't concern us, right?"

She slumped. "I suppose."

"Don't fret, little sister," Loyal said as he wrapped a reassuring arm around her shoulders. "Don't forget, Miss D.'s policeman friend said they're going to track down the figures. Someone's got them, for sure."

Jacob's Crossing was a pretty big place. She didn't know how the deputy was ever going to find them. "Do you think they'll have any luck?"

"I do. God has to be on our side for this case," Graham said. "Try not to worry. And don't forget how all those people volunteered to stand in for the real figures on Christmas Eve. Somehow, someway, we'll have a display here on the library front lawn."

"But it won't be perfect."

"It doesn't need to be," Graham admonished. "And try not to forget that what really matters is the real Jesus, and our faith and love for Him and each other. Those are the things to be thinking about right now."

Katie knew her brothers were right. But all the same, she

couldn't help but think that there was enough room in her heart to yearn for a better Christmas display.

But she'd just about given up on trying to get everyone to see how important it was to her. "So, are we going to leave now?"

"Of course not," Graham said. "Loyal and me said we'd help you sand and repaint the crèche, and that's what we're going to do."

"Even if Mary's gone missing?"

"When Mary shows up, she's going to need a place to be, right? And the English girl who's going to take her place on Christmas Eve needs a place to stand. Ain't so?"

Feeling better, Katie nodded. "May I help?"

"You may," Loyal replied. "Go ask Miss Donovan if she minds if we move the crèche onto the cement, over by the covered entrance. I want to have somewhere relatively dry to set the crèche on. This wet, snowy grass won't do."

"I'll ask her." She scampered in, anxious to hear the latest about the librarian's romance, too.

Miss D. was on the phone, so Katie walked through the book stacks until she located her aunt. But what she saw stopped her in her tracks. Instead of finding Ella chatting with children, or carefully shelving books, Katie spied her aunt down one of the book stacks, leaning against a shelf, grimacing in pain.

"Ella!" she cried out, running toward her.

"Shh!" an old, gray-haired lady whispered.

Ignoring her, Katie rushed past all the people glaring

at her until she got to her sister-in-law's side. "Ella, what's wrong? Are you hurt?"

Little by little, the lines right above Ella's glasses smoothed. "Katie, God bless you! I had begun to think I was going to have to call out for help. Go get Loyal, wouldja?"

Katie stepped a little closer, so close that if she reached out, she could touch Ella's hand. "What's wrong? Are you hurt? Is the baby sick?"

As if she was struggling to talk, Ella said slowly, "I don't want to talk now, child. Go do what I say. Get Loyal."

Never had Ella talked to her like that. Frightened, Katie nodded, then ran out the door, not even pausing when another elderly woman reprimanded her for running.

Both of her brothers looked up when she raced out the steps.

"Watch out, Katie," Graham warned. "If you're not careful, you're going to—"

"It's Ella, Loyal!" she interrupted. "Something's terribly wrong! She asked me to come get you."

His face paled. "Is it the baby?"

"I don't know. She just told me to go get ya. But she does look like she's hurting something awful."

Without another word, Loyal raced inside.

Graham dropped the bag of paint supplies he was holding and strode forward, a worried expression on his face. "We better go see if we can help."

"Uh huh. Ella's in the stacks. He won't know where to find her if I don't show him."

He gripped her hand. "Lead the way, *glay shveshtah*. Let's

go." Katie loved it when Graham called her "little sister" in Pennsylvania Dutch. It made her feel like the most important person in the world. Which right now, she was.

WHEN JAYNE SPIED Loyal, Graham, and Katie Weaver dashing across the main entryway, then calling Ella's name, she promptly hung up the phone and rushed over to help. The sight she found nearly took her breath away. Her friend was looking pale and scared, and her husband had his arm around her shoulders and was speaking softly to her. "Ella, what can I do?"

Her friend peered through her glasses with wide, frightened eyes. "I fear that the baby's coming early, Jayne. My water broke."

"We need to get you to the hospital."

She was just about to offer to drive them when Connor appeared at the end of the book stack.

"Hey," he said. "Boy, talk about perfect timing! The moment I walked inside, one of the assistants told me where you all were. I can drive y'all." He held up his cell phone. "Or would you rather have an ambulance? I can call for one right now."

"*Nee!*" Ella cried. "I'll be okay in just a car. But let's go."

As Loyal wrapped an arm around Ella's waist and Graham grabbed her purse, Connor, Jayne, and Katie followed behind.

"Connor, your timing continues to be perfect," Jayne said. "You really are the perfect guy to have in a crisis."

"I'm glad I'm here." He leaned close enough for her to smell his spicy aftershave. "Actually, I only stopped by to see if you wanted to go to dinner tonight."

"So soon?" she teased.

"I didn't see you on Sunday, so it's been two whole days."

"Practically forever."

"I can't seem to stay away from you," he quipped with a boyish smile.

"I'd love to join you."

"Great. I'll stop by when I get back from the hospital." He smiled, then rushed forward to help Loyal with the door to his truck.

Gazing at Ella, Jayne decided she seemed calmer. Ella was chatting softly to Graham while Loyal was helping her with her cloak.

The men seemed more at ease now, too.

Actually, the one person who looked to be really frightened was Katie. Jayne's heart softened as she noticed Katie's eyes had filled with tears and her bottom lip was trembling. After glancing Connor's way again, Jayne stepped to the little girl's side. "She'll be all right, Katie."

"I hope so."

As Loyal guided her forward, Ella turned back with a start. "Jayne, I almost forgot to ask. May Katie stay with you for a bit?"

Katie's shook her head. "*Nee!* I want to come, too."

"I know you do, but now is not the right time for you to be at the hospital."

"But—"

As Ella breathed through another contraction, Graham said, "Katie, I promise, if the baby comes soon, I'll drop back by and pick you up."

Seeking to distract her, Jayne added, "While we're waiting, you can help me organize the Christmas books."

Katie still didn't look too happy, but she nodded. "All right."

Jayne rested her hands on Katie's shoulders as Connor ushered Ella, Loyal, and Graham into the truck. When it was just the two of them left, Katie looked up at her. "Miss D., are you scared for Ella?"

Jayne figured it was best to be honest. "A little bit."

"Me too."

"That's okay. There's nothing wrong with that. But you know what? It won't help Ella or her baby if we just stand here and worry."

"So you think we should go sort books?" Katie asked.

"Yes, and pray for Ella and the baby."

"Okay," she began, then looked at Jayne with such a look of worry that it stopped her in her tracks. "Oh, Miss D., I think I've really messed up!"

"And why is that?"

"Because I've already been praying for something. I've been praying all the time for the nativity. Do ... do you think God still wants to hear from me? Maybe I've been asking for too much."

Truly, only Katie Weaver could make a person chuckle at a time like this. "I am sure God still wants to hear from you. He loves to hear from all of us, all the time, about any topic."

"Even when I keep asking Him for things?"

"Especially then. Listen, one of my favorite Scripture verses is from Isaiah. It says, '*Then when you call, the Lord will answer. "Yes, I am here," he will quickly reply.*'"

Katie's brows snapped together. "Even to me?"

"Uh huh. Let's go into my office and have some juice, then we'll pray, and then we'll go look at books. Okay?"

When Katie nodded, Jayne gave her a hug. And started praying. Though she didn't dare tell Katie, she didn't think Ella looked well at all.

She truly hoped both Ella and the baby were going to be all right.

Chapter Ten

· · · · · · · · ·

AT THE HOSPITAL, Ella felt like she was the eye in the center of a hurricane. All around her, people were busy, poking and prodding her, talking to each other, turning on machines.

She, on the other hand, felt completely still. Perhaps that was because she was still having a difficult time understanding her doctor's news. Turning to her husband, who was trying both to comfort her and to stay out of everyone's way, she whispered. "I can't have this baby today, Loyal. I'm not ready. We're not ready."

He chuckled. "I don't think the baby cares, dear. He or she intends to come into the world now."

She thought about that as another contraction hit her hard. When the pain eased, she said, "I hope it's okay."

"The *doktah* said nothing's wrong. It's just the baby's time, Ella."

That was true. But she couldn't help but fret. "Loyal, all

this time, I've never worried about his health or mine. But maybe something's wrong? What are we going to do if something is wrong?"

"If something is wrong, there are doctors who will help us. That's why we decided to come to the hospital, right?"

Nervously, she nodded. After seeing how the doctors and nurses had helped to heal Mattie's cancer, she and Loyal had opted for a hospital birth instead of a home one. "We will make the best of anything that happens."

Her husband's gaze softened as he kissed her brow. "Don't borrow trouble, Ella. You heard what the *doktah* said—he said everything looks fine."

"But it's early—"

"We might have gotten the dates wrong," he interjected smoothly. "Or maybe our baby intends to be a Christmas baby after all."

"Who ever heard of a baby being born so close to Christmas Day?"

Loyal's smile grew. "A fairly famous one."

"Oh, I know." She sighed, just as another contraction came. After breathing as the nurses reminded her to do, she said, "It's just . . . I wasn't prepared for this!"

"It doesn't matter, Ella. You'd better get prepared, then."

She choked back a laugh just as the nurses came back in.

"Time to leave the room for a few minutes, Dad," a nurse in a pair of pink scrubs said to Loyal. "We need to get your wife more settled."

For the first time, Loyal looked worried. "But—"

"It will only be a few moments."

Ella breathed hard and tried to look calm. "I'll be all right. Ask Graham to go home and tell the family. I'm going to want your mother here right quick."

"*Jah. Jah*, I can do that." He turned on his heel.

The nurse laughed. "Good for you, Ella. Give your husband things to do. Works every time."

As the nurse helped her take out the pins on her dress, Ella tried to keep a brave face. She didn't want to worry Loyal any longer. Surely, the nurses wouldn't be so cheery if they were worried, too.

But even so, she decided to privately start praying for their baby. Ella knew she could take any kind of pain or discomfort, as long as their baby that they'd wanted so much was healthy.

AFTER DROPPING OFF Graham, Loyal, and Ella, Connor stopped back by the library to give Jayne and Katie an update. Just as he was about to walk through the library's front door, he spied two cans of paint. They were sitting side by side, with a pair of paint brushes laid neatly on top of them. That looked like trouble to him. With all the shenanigans going on with the nativity set, those cans and paintbrushes were practically an invitation for someone to cause more mischief.

He'd just picked up a can of paint when Katie spied him through the front window. Right away, she opened the door. "How's Ella?"

"The doctors and nurses are taking good care of her. She seems excited about the baby."

"She's okay then?"

"Very okay."

Stepping forward, she pointed to the paint and brushes in his hands. "What are you doing?"

"Picking these things up so no one will use them to get into trouble."

"Oh, that paint is from my brothers," she said. "For the stable."

"The stable?"

"Uh huh." She pointed to the dwindling nativity set. "They were going to paint the crèche today. To try to make it look better. Even though, you know . . . pretty much everyone has gone missing."

Connor noticed Katie had lost some of her drive to create the best nativity ever. Instead, she sounded more than a little put out. And that made him a little sad.

Every child should have her innocence for as long as possible, and he hated the thought of her losing hers because of a string of unusual thefts at Christmas.

Though he didn't have a ton of experience with kids, he gave cheering her up a try. "I'm really sorry that someone keeps taking the figurines. Sometimes, people do things that don't make any sense, and that's hard to understand."

Katie blinked. "What do you do then?"

"Take a deep breath and do my job. I promise, I have been trying to figure out who's taking them." It just happened that there were precious few clues—and a whole lot more important things to worry about than a diminishing nativity set.

Her owlish gaze pinned him for a moment, just as if she

was trying to read his mind. Then, with a shrug, she sighed. "It's all right if you don't figure it out, I guess. I'm beginning to think that my *mamm* was right, anyway. She said I shouldn't be caring about an old plastic set of Mary and Joseph."

"I, for one, am glad you do! Why, someone needs to. If a group of plastic figures ever needed a guardian angel, I would say it's this set."

"And that's me?" She looked a little stunned by that. And, perhaps, a little bit proud, too.

"I think so." He smiled gently. "After all, if not for you, I don't think anyone would really care all that much. I would have tried to figure out who hurt Mrs. Jensen, then forgot about the nativity here on the library's lawn."

"Mamm said that a hurt lady is far more important than a missing plastic lamb."

"I'd have to agree with her. But my shift ended, so now I have time to worry about both." Fingering the paintbrush again, he said, "So, where were your brothers going to paint the stable?"

"Right here at the front door. We were going to ask Miss D. when we found out about Ella." Her bottom lip trembled. "Now Ella's scared and in the hospital and I have to stay here out of the way."

"I think they were more concerned with you not sitting in the hospital for the next several hours. They didn't want you to be bored. Babies can take a while to be born, you know."

"How do you know?"

Well, Katie Weaver was nothing if not blunt. "Because I have two sisters, and those sisters have had babies."

"You're an uncle?"

"Yep. Three times over." He looked at her proudly. "One niece and two nephews."

"I'm already an aunt, my brother Calvin already has a baby. But now I'm going to be an aunt of two babies."

"That's pretty special."

Her little chin rose a bit. Then she bit her lip. "So, did everything turn out okay with your sisters?"

"Yep." He rubbed the back of his neck. Boy, he hadn't thought about his sisters and the hours he'd kept his phone close while he'd waited to hear about their deliveries for quite a while. This year he hadn't been able to take any time off his new job, so he'd had to make do with sending packages to his nephews and niece.

Looking at Katie Weaver, he realized just how much he missed them. "You know, I've got some time right now. How about we go ahead and paint the stable?"

"You can do that?"

"Well, yeah. You might be surprised about this, but I can do more than just attempt to find thieves. I can paint things, too."

To his delight, she giggled.

"I'll get started. Why don't you go tell Miss D. what we're doing?"

When she scampered back inside, he carefully walked down the hill and started pulling the wooden structure back up it. The thing was heavier than it looked. By the time he was halfway, he'd tossed his jacket and gloves on the ground and was unzipping his fleece vest.

Two Amish men, their arms laden with books, stopped and watched his progress, their gazes solemn. One with a rather long gray beard looked particularly intrigued. "What are you doing, English? Stripping on the library's front lawn?"

"Only my jacket and gloves," he said with a laugh. "Actually, I thought I'd help out Katie Weaver and paint the crèche for her. Her brothers are at the hospital."

"Oh no. Someone in trouble?"

"Only of the good kind. Ella Weaver's baby is on the way."

Both men grinned. "Loyal's going to be having a time of it, I'm thinking. He's a calm sort, except when things aren't going so calmly."

Connor chuckled. "I'm beginning to get that same idea."

The younger Amish man stepped forward. "Do you have the paint?"

"Yep, it's right here. Loyal left it by the door."

"Want some help?"

The structure wasn't all that big—maybe six feet tall and four feet wide. It was really just a simple wooden frame. It wouldn't take more than an hour to paint it.

But that wasn't the point. Men in the community were reaching out to him. And he was so grateful for their outreach, there was no way he was going to push them away.

"I'd love some help. Thanks."

And with that, the younger of the two men trotted down the hill, picked up the crèche without as much as a grunt, and easily carried it up the hill. Connor couldn't help but be impressed. He wasn't a small man, and he worked out regularly. "Impressive," he mumbled under his breath.

The older guy heard him. "Farming," he said. "Bales of hay are heavy. Heavier than they look."

"I guess so."

When they parked the crèche in front of the door, Jayne met them with some old newspapers. "Katie just told me what you are doing. She's so excited about this. Thank you."

"It's nothing." Looking at the stack of newspapers in her hands, he asked, "So, are those for us?"

"Yep. Spread them out on the cement, just in case you drip."

"Thanks. And Jayne?"

"Yes?"

"Are we still on for dinner later?"

"Absolutely, if I'm not still watching Katie."

"Sounds good." He couldn't resist smiling as she turned and walked back inside. Suddenly, he felt warm and happy. Even the chilly temperatures didn't seem to affect him.

"Stop your mooning, English," one of the men said.

"Sorry. She, uh, said she'd go out to dinner with me tonight."

The other men chuckled. "A Christmas romance, hmm?" one said. "There's only one solution for what ails ya."

"And what is that?"

"Painting."

Connor grinned right back, then the three of them got to work. Katie came out, and stood to one side, watching it all with a look of contentment.

Within twenty minutes, however, one would have thought that they were creating a beautiful masterpiece instead of simply painting a wooden frame black. A crowd had formed around them.

People started asking questions about the crèche, about Ella, and about the nativity thief. He answered what he could. Katie—being Katie—fielded most of the questions. She told them how even though she wasn't supposed to care about the nativity, she did. And that a couple of people had volunteered to fill in for the spots on Christmas Eve.

"Do you need any more help?" one college-aged girl asked.

"*Jah*," Katie said. "It would be *wunderbaar* to have enough people to stand in for the whole nativity."

"Will you be wanting real animals, too?"

"If we can get 'em. It's only right, ain't so?"

The old man chuckled. "Katie Weaver, sometimes I can only imagine what your father is saying, looking down from heaven."

Her mouth formed a small O. "Do you think he'd be upset, Mr. Coblentz? My *mamm* says I'm incorrigible, you know."

"I don't know if you're incorrigible or not. But I do think your *daed* would be as proud as punch, Katie. You are doing a *gut* thing, caring about this nativity like you are."

Somewhat shyly, she tucked her chin to her chest.

As more people volunteered to help out, Connor realized that some organization was needed. "If some of you really do want to help Katie out, we should probably write all this down."

Then, to his amusement, Jayne got involved, too. She'd been quietly listening from the door of the library.

"I brought out some notepaper. Those who are serious about helping out, come over here, and let me write your name down."

At least seven people darted her way, just as the men finished painting the crèche.

Then, little by little, everyone went on his way, either back into the library, or down the sidewalks. At last, it was only he, Jayne, and Katie. The sudden silence, combined with the sense of satisfaction he felt from completing a job well-done, made him feel like words were unnecessary.

After a bit, Katie tugged on Jayne's sweater.

Jayne bent down. "Yes?"

"Are you happier now, Miss D.?" Katie asked.

Straightening up, she sent a Connor a perplexed look. "What are you talking about?"

When Katie motioned for Jayne to bend down again, Connor stepped to one side, to afford them at least the illusion of privacy.

"You know," Katie hissed into Jayne's ear—though not very quietly. "Are you happier about your love life?"

Connor didn't know whether he was more stunned by the question, or amused by the way Katie's question made Jayne's fair complexion turn a rosy red.

Jayne straightened abruptly. "Oh my word."

"Well, are you?" Katie asked.

After a quick glance his way, Jayne nodded. "Um, yes. Now, are you hungry? Because I need to take you down to the Kaffi Haus, and supposedly your uncle John has saved you an apple fritter."

"He did?"

"Um hum. Someone just called from his coffee shop. Your Uncle John is going to watch you until your mother gets home from the hospital."

Pure pleasure lit Katie's cheeks. "I'll go get my tote bag."

Jayne chuckled. "Take your time, dear. And don't forget your coat."

When they were alone, Connor couldn't resist teasing her. "So, you were sad about your love life, but not any longer?"

"Oh my goodness, I am definitely not going there with you."

"I just want to know if you are happier . . ."

"Don't start trying to interpret Katie. I promise, she blurts everything that's on her mind—to everyone and anyone. Conversations with her are not for the faint of heart."

At the moment, he was mentally giving thanks for Katie and her chatty nature. "Come now, Jayne. Tell me. All you need to do is tell me yes or no."

She bit her lip, and she looked so flustered and cute, he was tempted to hug her right there on the library's front steps. "In that case . . . yes."

"You make me happy, too." He didn't even try to temper his grin. "Especially since we can have our date since you won't need to watch Katie. Pick you up at your house at seven thirty?"

"That's fine."

"Great. I better get on my way, but I'll call you later."

"Hey, Connor?"

"Yeah?"

She waved a hand, signifying the crèche, the people that had gathered there . . . the list of volunteers for the Christmas Eve nativity. "Thanks for this."

"You're welcome. But we both know all I did was show up."

"You did more than that. And we both know that, too."

Chapter Eleven

· · · · · · · · ·

A YEAR AGO, Jayne had promised herself that she'd never enter the Kaffi Haus unless she was starving and there wasn't another place to eat within twenty miles. She'd been that reluctant to be around John Weaver.

But now things had changed.

Here she was, walking with Katie, holding hands, and chatting about babies and farm animals, of all things. It turned out that Katie knew quite a bit about sheep and lambs, and she was determined to share every bit of her knowledge.

"No, I didn't know that sheep liked to eat apples."

"They do," Katie said. "Cherries, too, though my brother Calvin said grass and a little bit of grain or corn is best for them."

"Katie, you are a fount of information."

She wrinkled her nose. "Is that *gut*?"

"Mighty *gut*," Jayne said with a smile.

All too soon, they were at the coffee shop and walking in. At the back of the shop, behind the counter that ran almost the whole width of the place, was John Weaver. The scene was almost exactly the same as when they'd first met.

"Katie, I've been waiting for you. Are you eager to be an aunt today?" he asked brightly, then colored as if he'd suddenly noticed who she was with. "Hello, Jayne."

"Hi, John." It was prideful, but she had to admit that she liked catching him off guard. Lord knew John's rejection of her had inspired many sleepless nights. "How are you?"

"I'm *gut*." His eyes darted to the door. Over her shoulder. Back to the counter he was polishing. Anywhere but directly at her. Then, if he'd just realized what he said, he rolled his eyes. "I mean, I'm fine."

"Even I know what *gut* means, John."

"I suppose that's true." He opened his mouth, then closed it again. Then, he walked around the counter and helped Katie off with her coat and gave her a warm hug.

Jayne stood to the side, content to take these moments to observe him a little longer. Though Jacob's Crossing was a very small town, she'd gone to extreme lengths to avoid him. Consequently, it had been quite a while since she'd taken a good long look at him.

He was still handsome.

Secretly, she was relieved her presence made him so uncomfortable. It made her realize that her hurt feelings hadn't been completely exaggerated. There really had been something between them—and he really had broken her heart.

John was dressed Amish now, of course. That had been one of the reasons he'd ultimately broken up with her. He'd chosen to marry an Amish woman who was a widow and return to his roots. Jayne had been terribly disappointed, especially because she'd known she couldn't compete with that.

A person's faith helped shape who he was. There was no way she could have encouraged him to betray who he was.

But even so, for a time she'd selfishly wished that she'd meant more to him than his faith. If human love could ever be more important.

But they'd all moved forward. Thankfully. "So, how is Mary? And Abel?"

His cheeks flushed. "Good. They're both good."

Bored with their conversation, Katie went around the counter until she was standing smack-dab in front of him. "Can I have a donut, Onkle John?"

"Of course you may!" He picked her up and gave her a little twirl. "That's why you came here, of course. Which one do you want?"

"An apple fritter?"

"Ah, yes. I do believe I have one apple fritter put aside for you. Go sit down and I'll bring it over." When she walked to a table, John pulled out a tissue wrapper and put one perfect donut on a plastic plate, then carried it out to her.

When he returned, he said, "Jayne, would you like one, too?"

It was his olive branch, she knew. And maybe olive

branches were worth the hundreds of calories that her waist-line didn't need. "I'd love a cake."

"You always did favor the plain ones."

"It's hard to find a perfect cake donut. I never had a better one than from right here."

"How about some coffee, too? It's fresh."

"Sure. But I'm afraid I need it to go. I need to get back to the library."

"We can do that."

After filling the paper cup and putting her donut in a white paper sack, he walked around the counter and handed both to her. "Here you go."

"Thanks." She reached into her jeans pocket and pulled out a five. "How much—"

"You don't need to pay, Jayne."

There had always been something about the way he said her name. The J sound was just a little bit soft, the long A just a little bit drawn out.

And upon hearing her name on his lips, she felt just a little bit breathless. Old habits, it seemed, died hard.

She needed to reinstate some distance.

"I think I do need to pay," she said firmly. She needed to remember that they didn't have a relationship. And that they never would again. Putting a new thread of brightness in her voice, she added, "You're running a business, right?"

"It's two fifty, then." He took her money and gave her the change.

She left fifty cents on the counter. "I'll see you later, Katie. I can't wait to hear what kind of baby Ella has."

"Me neither," she said around a bite.

"We're going to stop by the hospital in a little while," John blurted. "Is your cell phone number the same? If so, I could call from the hospital and give you an update."

"Thanks. I'd really appreciate it."

"It's no trouble I know you two are close friends."

"Thanks, John," she repeated, this time a little easier.

"Anytime."

She looked at him a little longer, then realized that the pain she kept expecting to feel wasn't there. Instead, she noticed that a glob of icing was smeared on Katie's cheek. The sticky substance coated a couple of her fingers, too. Hopefully, John would notice and hand her a couple of napkins, fast.

But more than that, she realized that it wasn't her place to do things like that any longer. While she once hoped to be an aunt to Katie, her favorite child, she had to remember: she was a good friend to Katie. Nothing more. "Goodbye, you two," she said, feeling like she was saying goodbye to a whole lot more than them for the afternoon.

She was saying goodbye to what could have been but now never would be.

Exiting the coffee shop, Jayne took comfort in the cold blast of air stinging her cheeks. The fresh breeze invigorated her and helped her shake off that last bit of melancholia.

But then she realized that there was now someone new in her thoughts. Someone whom she happened to have quite a bit in common with, and who also made her pulse race a bit.

And he was looking forward to seeing her later that evening.

There was something to be said for moving on, after all.

TWO HOURS LATER, when they got to the hospital, Katie's world turned dark. After signing in, she and Uncle John had taken the elevator to the third floor, then were shown to a waiting room for family members by the maternity ward. Everywhere Katie looked, there seemed to be big stainless carts filled with machines and linens and towels. Lots of women and men were everywhere, too, bustling around, looking extremely busy. Most wore green or pink loose outfits. But what she noticed the most was the pungent odor of disinfectant and bleach.

"It smells funny in here, Onkle," she whispered.

"I know. It's supposed to," he said as they walked through the waiting room's doorway.

Right away, Katie spied Mattie and Graham and Lucy and Calvin. "Where's Mamm and Loyal?"

"With Ella," Lucy said.

"Oh."

Tension was in the air, but Katie didn't understand why. She'd have thought it would be a time for smiles. Seeking comfort, she slid her hand into her uncle's softly calloused one.

He gave her hand a squeeze before turning to the rest of the family. "How is Ella doing?"

After a glance in Lucy's direction, Calvin answered. "She's having a time of it, I'm afraid."

"What's wrong?" her uncle asked, a line of worry forming between his brows.

Calvin started to speak, looked at her, then cleared his throat. "Katie, you'd best go sit down. I need to speak to John privately. Come out into the hall, John."

Katie tightened her grip on John's hand. "But I want to hear, too."

Calvin shook his head. "Not this time, Katie. This isn't news for your ears." When she opened her mouth to argue, his expression turned hard. "Go sit by Graham now."

Only Calvin could speak to her like that. It seemed when their *daed* passed away, each of them took over a different part of raising her. Loyal was the best at talking about feelings and giving hugs. As the youngest son, Graham drove her places in the buggy and laughed and played games with her.

Calvin? He was the one person she could always count on. He remained firm and solid and strict with her, which was both a good and bad thing. She trusted him like no one else, and because of that, she didn't try to sway him to her way of thinking very often.

With regret, she let go of her uncle's hand and sat down next to Graham, Mattie, and Lucy.

But she wanted to make sure Calvin knew she wasn't happy about it. She kept a frown on her face as she shifted and squirmed in one of the light blue chairs near the hallway as she watched Calvin and her uncle talk. Uncle John's expression turned worried, then his mouth looked pinched when he looked her way.

At last, after a brief hug, Calvin went back to Lucy, who

was hovering near the doorway, and John walked back to her. Without a word, he took the chair on her right.

Normally she would have pestered him with questions. But now all she wanted to do was have this moment last a little longer. Then she could keep pretending that everything was going to be fine.

Feeling worry flit through her, she squirmed a bit. Listened to the ticking of the big white clock over the quiet television.

After a couple of seconds, he looked her way. "Well, it's like this, Katie. Ella's blood pressure is getting a little high and the baby of hers doesn't seem to be in much of a hurry to meet the rest of us."

"What does that mean?"

"It means we have two choices. We can go back to Mary and Abel and wait for the new baby there, or we can wait here."

"If we go back to your *haus*, how will we know what is happening? You don't have a phone, do you?"

"No. We'd, uh, just have to wait for Calvin or Graham to stop by."

"But that could be a really long time." It already was hard sitting in her chair, waiting for John to tell her news.

"Yes, but at least you'd be out of the hospital waiting area." He folded his arms across his chest. "It might be best, all things considered."

"Why is that?"

"You wouldn't have to be sitting quietly for hours. You'd be able to sit with Mary, maybe play a game with Abel. Have a snack."

Katie realized that her uncle John and Calvin didn't think she would be able to sit quietly here.

Usually, she wouldn't. But this was Ella, whom she loved so very much. And because of that, she didn't want to go anywhere. "I want to stay here."

"Are you sure? I mean it, Katie. You won't be able to do much of anything. Just sit here." His voice lowered. "And none of us is going to be able to entertain you much."

She wasn't a baby any longer! She pointed to the television perched on a shelf in the corner of the room. "I'll be fine. There's a television in here."

"It's on *SportsCenter*. Not a cartoon show. You're going to be bored."

"Onkle John, I don't want to leave Ella. I'll be good, I promise."

He looked relieved. "All right then." He picked up an old magazine. "So now, we wait."

Relief flowed through her, making her feel like a wet noodle. Curling her legs underneath her, she got more comfortable, and watched the black hands on the white clock above the doorway slowly inch around the dial.

A whole hour passed. Loyal came out.

They all stood up, anxious. Not a one of them said a word, just looked and waited.

Then, to her surprise, Loyal walked right over in front of her and crouched down. "Katie, I heard you were out here. And being awfully quiet, too. I'm proud of you."

"I've been trying my best." She bit her lip. She wanted to ask how Ella was doing, she wanted to ask about Ella's baby too, but she was afraid. Was her brother trying to find a way to tell her that something was terribly wrong?

"Katie's been a *gut* girl, we're all mighty proud of her," John said. "But I'm afraid I'm going to be the one asking pesky questions now. How is Ella? How is your baby?"

Loyal looked to be gathering his thoughts, then, after clearing his throat, he spoke. "The doctor says if the baby doesn't come within the next hour, he wants to operate. Ella is in a lot of pain, and her blood pressure is rising." He bit his lip before glancing at them all. "I have to admit that this has been a mighty difficult day. It's hard to watch my Ella in so much pain."

"What can we do?" John asked.

"Pray. Please, just pray," Loyal said simply before turning around and walking back down the hallway.

Katie felt her lip tremble. She bit it, but all that did was cause her tears to start falling faster.

Onkle John noticed and reached for her hand. "Katie, I've always thought you had a real close relationship with our Lord. We need to pray for Ella and her *boppli*, okay?"

"Okay," she whispered. She didn't understand why her uncle thought she had a special relationship with God, but she did understand what it meant to pray real hard.

And then she remembered what she'd been praying for every night: a perfect nativity. She'd prayed and wished and asked God to let the nativity be perfect, because then her Christmas would be perfect, too.

She'd ignored Miss D.'s wishes, deciding that Miss Donovan needed to be happier in order to give Katie what she wanted.

She'd been wrong.

She'd ignored her mother's reminders, about how Christmas wasn't about decorations or fancy Christmas plays or "real" nativities. It was about celebrating Jesus's birth, and giving thanks for all the blessings and love in their lives. Katie hadn't really believed that, though. She'd been sure there was more to it than her mother's simple explanations.

She'd been wrong.

She'd even asked Ella and her brothers to help her get her way . . . because she was used to getting her way. She was used to being a spoiled girl.

The tears fell harder and her nose started to run, too.

"Ach, Katie, don't cry, sweetheart." Onkle John handed her a white handkerchief. "Ella will be all right. The doctors and nurses are helping her. I promise, they are. Even though this hospital seems like a scary place, it's the best spot for her. Loyal was smart to insist that she have the baby with doctors and nurses nearby."

"I know."

"Gott has helped me through some mighty difficult days," Lucy said, her sweet voice floating through the room like a soothing balm. "He was with me when Timmy was born, and He'll be here for Ella now, just like He's been with her all along. Try to remember that, dear."

"I will." Katie wanted to say more, but she didn't dare. Everything she was feeling was so new and scary, she knew she wouldn't be able to explain it to her uncle in just the right way.

Instead, she brought her feet up on the chair and curved her arms around her knees. Then she tucked in her face, closed her eyes up tight, and started talking to God in earnest.

"I finally understand," she whispered. "I know now what Christmas is all about. It's about family and love and Ella being safe. It's about being happy with what you already gave us. It's about thinking about what other people want instead of myself. It's about you, God."

She hiccupped into her skirts and waited for Him to talk back. But all she felt was her uncle John's hand on her back, gently rubbing circles around her shoulder blades.

She closed her eyes and kept praying. She prayed as hard as she could, and then when she said everything she could think of, she snuggled closer to her uncle's side and let herself relax.

There was nothing to do now but wait.

Just as Katie was starting to feel drowsy, leaning into her uncle John, she felt him tense as he dropped the magazine he was reading and sat up straight. "What's happening?" he asked.

Katie peeked and saw Loyal had come back. His eyes looked tired, and he looked kind of sweaty, too.

She sat up and stared.

When he met her eyes, he curved one hand, motioning her toward him.

She scooted off the chair and walked toward him with shaky knees. To her surprise, the moment she stood right in front of him, he knelt down, kissed her forehead, and then hugged her tight. "You have a niece, Katie," he said, his voice so happy and pleased that it sounded like melted butter on warm toast.

She pushed out of his embrace. "And Ella?"

"Ella is fine, too." He rocked back on his heels so he could see her face. Then smiled so bright. "They're both fine. Better than fine. They're *wunderbaar*! I promise."

"I'm glad."

Behind her, Lucy and Mattie and Graham and Calvin and John were all cheering. "Don't be shy, Loyal. Tell us the news. How much does she weigh? What's her name?"

"Our daughter is a perfect seven pounds, four ounces, and twenty inches in length," he stated. "She has blue eyes and lovely blond, wispy hair. And . . ." he added, with a meaningful look at Katie, "her name is Katherine Weaver."

Everyone else gasped and then cheered.

Katie smiled, too, but she really only felt relief. Ella was okay. And her baby was, too! God had answered her prayers!

With a creak and a groan, Loyal got to his feet, smiling softly at her all the while. "Katie, you don't understand why Ella named her baby Katherine, do you?"

She shook her head. Did it even matter?

"She named our little girl after someone special. After a certain Katherine she is mighty fond of. A Katie who she loves very much."

"She did?" Loyal's words hardly made sense. Could she really mean so much to Ella? It didn't seem possible.

Leaning a little bit closer, Loyal said, "Ella named our baby after you, Katie Weaver. The baby is your namesake."

"I'm that special?"

"Yes, *shveshtah*. You are that special, indeed."

Katie thought about saying something, but she had no more words in her head. All she could think about was that Ella was okay, and that God loved her so much that He gave her a little girl, a little niece to take care of and play with.

For some reason, the tears came back. But this time, they were happy tears. Giving in to temptation, she wrapped her arms around Loyal and hugged him tight.

With a chuckle, Loyal hugged her right back, just as if he never intended to let her go.

Chapter Twelve

· · · · · · · · · ·

AFTER MUCH DEBATE, Connor decided to take Jayne to the Dutch Inn for dinner. They specialized in Amish home cooking, and since the Amish were such a big part of the Geauga County community, he figured they might as well enjoy the specialties of the area.

But though she'd agreed to his choice, he noticed that she barely looked at the menu and didn't seem to be all that happy to be in the restaurant. He couldn't understand why—until she told him her reason.

"Last year, I dated an Amish man. It wasn't really serious, but I really liked him."

"I didn't know the Amish dated outsiders."

"Well, it's complicated. His name is John Weaver. He's, uh, Katie's uncle. He never joined the order. He left when he was eighteen and lived in Indianapolis for twenty years. But then his brother died and he wanted to be there for his brother's family. When we dated, he didn't intend to return to his childhood faith. But then he did."

"Wow. So, he's still around?" With a bit of a shock, he realized that he was feeling jealous. Mentally, he shook his head. He needed to concentrate on keeping his expression schooled and open. Jayne needed to know that she could trust him to be a good listener.

"Yes. He owns the Kaffi Haus."

"Wow," he said again. "I've been in there a lot. And I've talked to . . . John, though I didn't know his name. He's a nice guy."

"Yes, he is." Looking a bit miserable, Jayne added, "Not too long after we broke things off, he married an Amish woman. I didn't mean to feel hurt, but I guess I did."

"I can understand that."

"Can you?" Her lips turned up slightly, as if she was pleased by the news. Then she took a sip of water. "So, that's why I'm not a big fan of Amish cooking," she said, looking a little flustered. "It's stupid, but it just seems to remind me of what I didn't measure up to. Aren't you glad you asked?"

He noticed that she looked embarrassed. "I'm glad you told me, but I'm sorry if was I asking you too many questions about something you didn't want to talk about. It's a bad habit of mine—the nature of the job, I'm afraid."

She reached out and pressed her hand against his. "Actually, I'm glad we talked about it. Not everyone knows we dated, but enough people do that I'd feel terrible if you found out about it from someone else."

"Are you okay now?"

"You know what? I think I am. I saw him today. I needed to drop off Katie. What I discovered was that the two of us are okay. We might never be good friends again, but I think enough time has passed for me to go to his coffee shop every now and then."

"And maybe one day you'll like broasted chicken. I mean, you don't have anything against chicken, do you?"

To his delight, she laughed. "Not a single, solitary thing. You're right, I need to give broasted chicken another try."

He flipped his hand over so that he could grasp hers more securely. This was nice, talking about their pasts, about things that mattered. Teasing her just enough to make her smile.

Still staring at their linked hands, she murmured, "So, Connor, have you ever been in a situation like mine?"

"Dating an Amish man? Never."

She chuckled. "Connor, you know what I mean."

"You're right, I do," he replied, turning more serious. "And the answer is no. I mean, not really. The last serious relationship I had ended when I decided to enter the police academy. My girlfriend didn't want to date a cop."

"I'm shocked! You're in such an honorable profession."

"I think so . . . but being a cop's wife wasn't the future she had in mind." Her rejection still stung, so he covered it up with a grin. "Don't know why—long hours, little pay . . . me spending my days dealing with drug addicts and criminals . . ."

As he'd hoped, she smiled. "Put that way—"

He shrugged. "The job is hard enough without having no support at home. It all worked out for the best. Some women don't want to date cops. Not even sheriffs or deputies."

"I don't mind it. Actually, I kind of like dating a deputy. Don't forget, my dad was a cop." Looking almost shy, she added, "You make me feel safe."

He squeezed her hand. "I was hoping you'd say that." He was going to say more when the door opened and Jayne lit right up. "Oh, excuse me, Connor," she said before she rushed over to the four newcomers.

Connor leaned back in his chair and watched her scurry over, exclaim, then start hugging both women and beaming at the men. Then she pointed at him. He waved.

"Let me introduce you," she said to her friends, then brought them over. Connor stood up when they approached.

"Connor, this is Lucy and Calvin Weaver, and Mattie and Graham Weaver. Ella is married to Calvin and Graham's brother."

He shook hands with them all. "Nice to meet you."

Jayne smiled. "Ella had a little girl! She's naming her Katherine after our little Katie."

He laughed. "That's wonderful news. Now, Katie I've definitely met."

One of the men shook his head in mock frustration. "Who hasn't met my little sister? She could run the whole town if she had her mind set on that."

Jayne shook her head. "She's not that precocious. Not yet, anyway."

"Well, congratulations to you all. Would you like to join us? We're just about to have coffee and pie."

"*Danke*, but we're only picking up pies to take home," Calvin said. "It's been a long evening."

When they left, Jayne grinned at him. "I'm so happy everything went well for Ella."

"Me too." He was about to say more when his phone beeped, just as his partner, Trey, wandered inside. "Connor, I thought that was your truck outside. Come on, if you can. We got problems."

He was already reaching into his pocket and pulling out his billfold. "What happened?"

"It's that darn nativity again."

Surely Trey hadn't come to get him because another plastic figure had been stolen? "What happened?"

"Well . . . it seems that another piece has gone missing . . . and was found on the property of Mrs. Jensen."

"Isn't she the woman who was injured?" Jayne asked.

"Yep," Trey answered. "And this little story gets even worse."

With a sinking feeling, Connor waited for the details. "What happened?"

"Someone came forward and told us that he'd actually seen Mrs. Jensen steal some of the nativity pieces. When we went to her house to ask her about it, she became a little argumentative, which made Jackson decide to walk her inside her home and out of the neighbors' sight, and that's when we entered the fun house." He sighed. "Connor, Sheriff Jackson discovered all kinds of stuff. She's some kind of kleptomaniac."

"A klepto?"

"A Christmas klepto. Jackson called me, and we discovered all the pieces. And then some. I guess she's been stealing

Christmas decorations and whatnot for years. Turns out she's kind of a Christmas hoarder."

The idea sounded sad and strange and just a bit outlandish, too. "I've never heard of such a thing," Jayne murmured.

"That would be two of us," Connor added.

Trey shook his head. "Guys, you should have seen her place. It would even put Santa Claus on medication. Her living room looks like a Christmas tree junkyard. I'm surprised she can even walk through the place."

"What about the figurines? Are they evidence? I'd kind of like them back," Jayne asked.

"I reckon we'll be able to give them to you without a problem. But I have to tell you, they're a little worse for wear." He wrinkled his nose. "She's got cats, too. Lots and lots of cats."

"Oh brother. I've got to do something. All I've got now is a painted crèche that's practically empty."

"You've got more than that," Connor reminded her. "Remember, everyone signed up to participate on Christmas Eve."

"Jayne, I'm sorry, but I've got to steal Connor from you. Currently, Mrs. Jensen is either yelling at our boss or crying. The neighbors have started to gather."

"I'll be right there, as soon as I take Jayne home."

"I'm ready. You've got police work to do."

Five minutes later, when they were in his car, she couldn't resist teasing him. "I tell you what, Connor. I can now see why that girl you were dating was so upset. You've got dangerous Christmas hoarders on the loose."

For a full thirty seconds he tried not to smile. Then he

let go and began laughing. Loud and proud. "It's not pretty, but I guess someone has to deal with this craziness. Is my job scaring you, Jayne?"

"I should be able to handle things . . . but only if you kiss me good night again . . . and promise to call me later and tell me what happened."

"I can do both of those things! I promise, your kiss is going to be the best part of the day. And I wouldn't want to share this story with anyone else."

Epilogue

· · · · · · · · · ·

Christmas Eve

NO ONE REALLY knew how hard it was to be Katie Weaver. Not Miss Donovan, who looked so in love that she hardly stopped making googly eyes at Deputy Fields.

Not Deputy Fields, 'cause even though he'd found all the nativity pieces, he hadn't found them in time to do much of anything besides deliver them to Miss D. And now they kind of smelled.

Mamm and Ella and Lucy and Mattie and her brothers seemed determined to be interested in only one thing: baby Katherine.

Which meant that making sure that Jacob's Crossing's first real live nativity was a success was all up to her.

Luckily, lots of people had volunteered to help her out. Onkle John had brought his wife's goat. Another farmer brought his donkey. And Mr. Miller had lent them two sheep. He'd even dressed up his kids like shepherds so the sheep didn't get too out of hand.

"Katie. Where do you want us?" Charlie asked, all dressed up in a white sheet.

"Angels in the back." She pointed to three other *Englisher*s. "You three kings, come on through and stand over by the goat."

And so it continued. Old people, young people, animals, and kids all had shown up in various costumes and were willing to listen to her tell them where to go.

Then finally it was all perfect, except for Mary and Jesus. "Where's the baby?" she asked, bracing herself to see the plastic baby Jesus who'd been sitting in storage forever.

"Here," she heard a voice behind her.

Ella stood there with her arms outstretched, baby Katherine in her arms.

"Ella, Mamm said you couldn't come outside! And especially not the baby."

Ella carefully lifted up Katherine's covering. "Loyal and I figured the cool air wouldn't hurt her if we didn't stay out too long."

"So, you'll be Mary and Jesus?"

"Yep." Ella turned and carefully went to the chair that Loyal had set up next to the manger. Katie watched Loyal help Ella sit down.

Then, Katie stood back. Looking at the pretty picture they'd created. Everyone looked a little silly, dressed up in mismatched costumes, and chattering away to one another.

And her uncle's goat seemed unable to resist chewing on a wiseman's flowered bedsheet.

Snow had fallen in the morning, and now a faint breeze lifted the air. Ella and Baby Katherine looked wonderful—even if the baby was a girl and not a boy like Jesus.

A little burst of happiness began to flow through Katie.

All the sudden, a couple of kids gathered in the watching crowd started singing "Silent Night." Then a couple more joined them. Pretty soon, everyone who was standing around was singing, people young and old, Amish and English.

Except for those in the crèche.

They simply stood. Looking perfect.

Katie's heart swelled.

Miss D. walked to her side, tears in her eyes. "You did it, Katie. You got everyone together, and we have a beautiful, beautiful nativity. It's the most wonderful nativity I've ever seen."

With a critical eye, Katie realized that Miss D. was right. Even though most people were only wearing towels and sheets, they looked just right. Even though there were folks of all ages, and some, like Ella, were wearing a *kapp*, they all fit together.

But what was really the best was that they were all there together. "I think it's the best, too," she said, feeling like God was smiling down on them.

"Hey, look!" someone shouted, pointing to the sky.

And sure enough, somehow the breeze had encouraged a

couple of clouds to part. Stars had come out. And more than a few looked especially bright.

So bright that they could lead other people to Jacob's Crossing, maybe.

Feeling like everything was about as perfect as it could be, Katie realized, suddenly, that being Katie Weaver was actually a very good thing.

"Merry Christmas!" Katie Weaver called out. "Merry Christmas, everyone!"

Standing next to her, her mother hugged her close. "Merry Christmas to you, Katie," she whispered. "And may God bless you. May God bless us all."

Sour Cream Cutout Cookies Recipe

· · · · · · · · ·

Ingredients for cookies:
- 1 cup shortening or oleo
- 1 cup brown sugar
- 2 eggs
- 1 tsp. vanilla
- 1 cup sour cream
- 5½ cups flour
- 2 tsp. baking powder
- 1 tsp. baking soda
- 1 tsp. salt

Ingredients for icing:
- 1 cup powdered sugar
- ¼ cup milk
- 1 tsp. vanilla

Directions: Cream shortening and sugar together. Add eggs, vanilla, and sour cream and mix. Add dry ingredients and mix well. Chill for several hours. Roll out and cut with your favorite cookie cutters.

Bake at 350 degrees Fahrenheit for about 8 minutes, or until set and lightly browned on the edges. Cool.

For icing, combine powdered sugar and milk. Mix until the icing is smooth and easy to spread. Add vanilla.

Make 3 – 4 dozen cookies, depending on the size of the cut-outs.

About the Author

· · · · · · · · ·

SHELLEY SHEPARD GRAY is the *New York Times* and *USA Today* bestselling author of the Families of Honor, Seasons of Sugarcreek, Sisters of the Heart, and Secrets of Crittenden County series. She lives with her family in southern Ohio, where she writes full-time. Her next series, Days of Redemption, launches in early 2013 with *Daybreak*.

www.shelleyshepardgray.com
www.facebook.com/ShelleyShepardGray

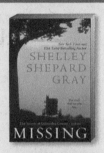

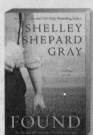